Leonardo Bufalini, Giambattista Nolli

A Description of Ancient Rome

containing a short account of the principal buildings, places, &c. noticed in

the annexed plan of that city, drawn from an actual survey

Leonardo Bufalini, Giambattista Nolli

A Description of Ancient Rome
containing a short account of the principal buildings, places, &c. noticed in the annexed plan of that city, drawn from an actual survey

ISBN/EAN: 9783337381394

Printed in Europe, USA, Canada, Australia, Japan

Cover: Foto ©Andreas Hilbeck / pixelio.de

More available books at **www.hansebooks.com**

OF

ANCIENT ROME,

CONTAINING

A SHORT ACCOUNT

OF THE

Principal BUILDINGS, PLACES, &c. noticed in the annexed Plan of that city, drawn from an actual furvey, by *Leonardo Bufalino*, in the year 1551; reduced to a fmaller fcale by *J. B. Nolli*, in 1748; and now republifhed : with references to the paffages in M. *Rollin's Hiftory of the Roman Republic*, and M. *Crevier's Hiftory of the Roman Emperors*, where they are mentioned.

LONDON,

Printed for JOHN KNAPTON:

And fold by ROBERT HORSFIELD in Ludgate-Street.

MDCCLXI.

For readily finding the

PRINCIPAL BUILDINGS, PLACES, &c.

OF

ANCIENT ROME,

Noticed in the annexed Plan of that City.

By defcending from the capital letters A, B, C, &c. at the top of this plan, to the correfponding letters at the bottom; and traverfing it from the Italic letters *a, b, c,* &c. at the fides; the eye will be guided to the fpot fought for.   For inftance : the *Colifeum,* marked in the article THEATRES and AMPHITHEATRES, with the letters DE. *e*; ftands between the letters D and E at the top of this plan, and overagainft the letter *e* at the fides.—The gate *Nomentana,* now *St. Agnes* (H. *c*), under the article GATES, will be found exactly where a line drawn down from H, and another a-crofs from *c,* would interfect each other.—The *Temple of Antoninus and Fauftina,* not expreffed by name in the body of the plan, but defignated in the fide references by the figures 284, and marked under the article TEMPLES (D. *de.* 284), will be found under the letter D, and between *d* and *e,* indicated in the plan by the figures 284.—And fo of the reft.

WE shall begin this explanation of the annexed plan of Rome, with the general division of that city into *wards* or *regions*, as collected by B. Kennett from the accurate Panvinius; and then range, under their respective alphabetical heads, the principal places and buildings mentioned therein; in order to facilitate the means of finding their several situations.

The Division of ROME into WARDS, or REGIONS.

Romulus divided his little city into three *tribes*[a]; and Servius Tullius added a fourth[b]; which division continued till the time of Augustus, who first instituted the fourteen *regions* or *wards*[c].

The FIRST REGION, called PORTA CAPENA (DF. *gb*), contained

9 Streets.	6 Public baths.
3 *Luci*, or consecrated groves.	4 Arches.
	14 Granaries.
4 Temples.	12 Mills for grinding corn.
6 *Ædes*, or sacred buildings.	121 *Domi*, or great houses.

The whole compass of this ward was 13223 feet.

---

[a] See Rollin's Rom. Hist. Vol. I. p. 23.   [b] Id. ibid. p. 50.
[c] See Crevier's Rom. Emperors, Vol. I. p. 219.

REGION

Region II. COELIMONTIUM (DF. *eg*).

12 Streets.
2 *Luci.*
5 Temples.
The public baths of the
    city.

80 Private baths.
The great shambles.
23 Granaries.
23 Mills.
133 Great houses.

The compass 13200 feet.

Region III. ISIS and SERAPIS (CD. *bc*).

8 Streets.
2 Temples.
The amphitheatre of Ves-
    pasian.
The baths of Titus, Tra-

jan, and Philip.
19, or, some say, 29 Gra-
    naries.
23 Mills.
160 Great houses.

The compass 12450 feet.

Region IV. VIA SACRA, or TEMPLUM PACIS (CE. *df*).

8 Streets.
10 Temples.
The colossus of the sun,
    120 feet high.
The arches of Titus, Se-

verus, and Constantine.
75 Private baths.
18 Granaries.
24 Mills.
138 Great houses.

The compass, according to some, only 8000; according to others, 14000 feet.

Region V. ESQUILINA (FH. *df*).

15 Streets.
8 *Luci.*
6 Temples.
5 *Ædes.*

75 Public baths.
18 Granaries.
22 Mills.
180 Great houses.

The compass 15950 feet.

Region VI. ACTA SEMITA (DE. *c. d*).

12, or 13 Streets.
15 Temples.
2 Porticos.
2 *Circi.*
2 *Fora.*

75 Private baths.
19 Granaries.
23 Mills.
155 Great houses.

The compass 15600 feet.

Region VII. VIA LATA (DE. *ac*).

40 Streets.
4 Temples.
75 Private baths.
3 Arches.

17 Mills.
25 Granaries.
120 Great houses.

The compass 23700 feet.

Region VIII. FORUM ROMANUM (CE. *de*).

12 Streets.
21 Temples.
66 Private baths.
10 *Ædes.*
9 Porticos.
4 Arches.
7 *Fora.*

4 *Curiæ.*
7 *Basilicæ.*
6 Columns.
18 Granaries.
30 Mills.
150 Great houses.

The compass 14876 feet.

Region IX. CIRCUS FLAMINIUS (AC. *ce*).

20 Streets.
8 Temples.
20 *Ædes.*
12 Porticos.
2 *Circi.*
4 Theatres.
3 *Basilicæ.*

2 *Curiæ.*
5 Baths.
2 Arches.
2 Columns.
32 Mills.
32 Granaries.
189 Great houses.

The compass 30560 feet.

REGION

Region X. PALATIUM (CE. *ce*).

7 Streets.
10 Temples.
9 *Ædes*.
1 Theatre.
4 *Curiæ*.

15 Private baths.
12 Mills.
16 Granaries.
109 Great houses.

The compass 11600 feet.

Region XI. CIRCUS MAXIMUS (D. *ef*).

8 Streets.
22 *Ædes*.
15 Private baths.

16 Granaries.
12 Mills.
189 Great houses.

The compass 11600 feet.

Region XII. PISCINA PUBLICA (DE. *fb*).

12 Streets.
2 *Ædes*.
68 Private baths.

28 Granaries.
25 Mills.
128 Great houses.

The compass 12000 feet.

Region XIII. AVENTINUS (CE. *eb*).

17 Streets.
6 *Luci*.
6 Temples.
74 Private baths.

36 Granaries.
30 Mills.
155 Great houses.

The compass 16300 feet.

Region XIV. TRANSTIBERINA (AC. *df*).

23 Streets.
6 *Ædes*.
136 Private baths.

20 Granaries.
32 Mills.
150 Great houses.

The compass 33409 feet.

ÆDES.

Æ D E S.

The *Sacred Ædes* of the Romans were buildings erected in honour of some particular deity, but not formally consecrated by the augurs : for if they afterwards received that consecration, they then changed their names to temples [d].

We find the following mentioned in this plan.

Ædes Romuli (CD. *de.* 276), near which stood the famous *Ficus Ruminalis*, or Fig-tree, under which Romulus and Remus were nursed, and which Tacitus [e] gravely tells us, lasted upwards of eight hundred years [f]. The *Ædes*, indeed, originally the cottage of the shepherd Fauftulus, in which the twin brothers were brought up, was preserved for many ages by order of the senate, and at last converted into, or rather taken in as part of, a temple sacred to Augustus.

Ædes Spei (D. *gh*) without the walls of Rome.

Ædes Augusti Tiberii (D. *e.* 278).

Ædes Virtutis (DE. *gh*).

The *Ædicula* of the Romans was only a diminutive, fignifying no more than a little *Ædes*.

Their *Sacellum*, which may be derived the fame way from *Ædes Sacra*, was, according to Festus, a place facred to the gods, without a roof.

The *Delubrum*, according to Servius, was a place which, under one roof, comprehended several deities.

The *Templum* was the principal place of worfhip.

Thefe were the general names of the buildings fet apart for religious purpofes, by the Romans.

[d] Agell. l. 14. c. 7.   [e] Annal. l. 13. c. 58.
[f] Rollin, Vol. I. p. 12.

DESCRIPTION OF
AQUEDUCTS.

The aqueducts of the Romans are juftly ranked among their nobleft and moft ufeful works. Sextus Julius Frontinus, a perfon of confular dignity, who lived in the reign of Vefpafian, and wrote a treatife exprefsly on this fubject, fays, they were one of the cleareft tokens of the grandeur of the empire [s]. Dionyfius Halicarnaffenfis [h] and Strabo [i] faw them in the fame light ; and add to them, as farther proofs of the amazing magnificence of the ftate, the *Cloacæ* or common fewers of Rome, and the high-ways.

The firft invention of aqueducts is afcribed to the cenfor Appius Claudius [k], who, in the year of Rome 441, brought water into the city by a channel eleven miles long. But this was little in comparifon of what was afterwards done by the emperors and others, feveral of whofe conduits were cut through mountains, rocks, and all forts of obftacles, for upwards of forty miles together. As to the *Cloacæ*, or common-fewers, they were of fuch an height, that, as Procopius fays [l], a man on horfeback might eafily ride through them, even in the ordinary courfe of the channel, the vault and arches of which were, in fome places, upwards of an hundred feet high [m].

Procopius [n] reckons only fourteen aqueducts in ancient Rome : but Victor [o] has enlarged the number to twenty. The moft remarkable of thofe, of which any traces now remain, are, as marked in the annexed plan,

Aqua Appia, the aqueduct of Appius juft mentioned as the oldeft of all, which conveyed water from

[s] For farther particulars concerning Frontinus, fee Crevier's Rom. Emperors, Vol. VI. p. 14, 356. and Vol. VII. p. 65.
[h] Lib. 3.
[i] Lib. 5.

[k] See Rollin's Rom. Hift. Vol. III. p. 208.
[l] De Bell. Goth. lib. 1.
[m] Sext. Jul. Frontin.
[n] De Bell. Goth. lib. 1.
[o] Defcript. Urb. Region.

Tufculum

Tufculum to the Capitol, and entered Rome near the *Porta Trigemina*, now St. Paul's Gate. BC. *fg.*

Aqua Augufta, called likewife *Alfietina* [p], from the lake of that name, about fourteen miles from Rome, near the Claudian Way, from whence it was brought. This water, being unwholfome to drink, was ufed chiefly for watering gardens and filling the *Naumachiæ*. It's conduit entered the city at the *Porta Efquilina*, now the Gate of St. Laurence. GH. *de.*

Aqua Claudia, reckoned the next in goodnefs to the *Aqua Marcia*, which was the beft of all. This aqueduct was begun by Caligula, and finifhed by Claudius, who brought it's waters from two fprings, called *Cæruleus* and *Curtius* [q], about thirty-fix miles diftant from Rome [r]. Vefpafian, Titus, Marcus Aurelius, and Antoninus Pius, repaired and extended it; as did alfo, in later times, the popes Sixtus V. and Paul V, and it now fupplies the fountain called *Felice*, built by the former of thefe pontifs near St. John Lateran. It enters the city at the *Porta Nævia*, now *Porta Maggiore*, or the *Gate of the Holy Crofs.* This was the higheft arched of all the aqueducts. DH. *ef.*

Aqua Marana : an open ftream, which runs from the gate *Gabiufa* to the *Tiber.* This, both Donatus and Nardini [s] take to have been the ancient *Aqua Crabra* and *Damnata*, which M. Agrippa cut off from all his aqueducts, on account of it's badnefs. How it has been fince brought to Rome, is not known : but even now it is not ufed for drinking. *fg.*

Aqua Marcia, likewife called *Aufelia*, faid to have been firft brought to Rome by the prætor Q. Marcius, from a fpring near the Valerian Way, upwards of thirty miles diftant from the city, which it enters near the *Efquiline* Gate [t]. This was, and ftill is, reckoned

[p] Donati, Roma Vetus ac Recens, lib. 3. & Frontin.
[q] Suet. in Claud. c. 20.
[r] Frontin.
[s] Donat. l. 3. & Nardini, Roma Antica. l. 8. c. 4.
[t] Frontin.

the

the beſt drinking water in Rome. M. Agrippa repaired this aqueduct, and laid pipes from it to ſeveral parts of the city. The *Aqua Marcia*; the *Aqua Julia*, which we ſhall ſpeak of next; and another water called *Tepula*, the ſource of which we know not; entered Rome in one and the ſame aqueduct, divided into three ranges or ſtories, in the uppermoſt of which ran the *Aqua Tepula*, in the ſecond the *Aqua Julia*, and in the loweſt the *Aqua Marcia*; all which were divided and diſtributed into different parts of the city, after their entrance, within the walls. This accounts for the extraordinary height of this aqueduct, which greatly ſurpaſſed that of any other in Rome. From the ruins of this fabric, which ſtill ſubſiſt, and are called *Il Caſtel del Acqua Marcia*[v], it plainly appears to have been a moſt ſuperb ſtructure; of which we have a farther proof in the two famous marble trophies, commonly called Marius's Trophies, which pope Sixtus V. removed, from two niches in this building, to the Capitol. GH. *e*.

Aqua Julia[w], brought to Rome from the *Campus Lucullus* near the *Via Latina*, twelve miles off, by M. Agrippa, in the year of Rome 721. It enters the city near the *Eſquiline* Gate, and had it's name, according to Frontinus, from one *Julius*, who firſt diſcovered the ſpring which ſupplies it. HI. *de*.

Aqua Virgo, (FI. *ab*) which enters Rome at the gate *Pinciana*. This water was brought thither by M. Agrippa, in the 735th year of the city; Caius Sentius and Spurius Lucretius being conſuls. It was called the *Virgin Water*, from it's ſpring being ſhewn by a little girl, to ſome ſoldiers who were at work near the Præneſtine road, about eight miles from Rome[x], where now is the ſource which ſupplies that vaſt and magnificent fountain called *la Fontana di Trevi*, built

[v] Elegantly drawn by *Piraneſi*, in his *Views of Rome*.
[w] Nardini, l. 8. c. 4.
[x] Frontin. & Nardini, l. 8. c. 4.

by that excellent architect Nicola Salvi, and finely reprefented by Piranefi in his views of Rome; where he
alfo takes notice of the

Meta Sudans, now only a rough unfhaped ftone,
but faid to have been formerly a fountain near the *Colifeum* (where it is marked in this plan), for the ufe of
the wreftlers and others, who frequented that amphitheatre. DE. *de.*

Numbers of other ancient aqueducts are now either
fo far loft, or blended with thefe, that antiquarians
have taken great pains, to little purpofe, in order to
trace their remains. But as fuch difquifitions, could
they be of any fervice, would carry us far beyond the
intended limits of this fhort account; we fhall conclude this article with obferving, that the *Fontana di
Trevi,* juft now mentioned; the *Fontana Felice,* built
by pope Sixtus V; and the *Fontana Paulina,* the
work of Paul III, fupply the prefent Rome abundant-
ly with water; and that the aqueducts of the ancients
were under the care and direction firft of the cenfors
and ediles, and afterwards of particular magiftrates,
called *Curatores Aquarum,* inftituted by the great A-
grippa, who made the perfecting of the aqueducts of
Rome a principal object of his attention[y]. The il-
luftrious Meffala was one of thefe *Curatores* in the
reign of Auguftus[z]; and Frontinus held the fame office in that of Nerva[a].

ARCHES (TRIUMPHAL).

The triumphal arches of the Romans were public
buildings, defigned for the reward and encourage-
ment of noble enterprizes, and erected generally to
the honour of fuch eminent perfons as had either gain-
ed a victory of extraordinary confequence abroad, or
refcued the commonwealth from any confiderable

[y] See Rollin's Rom. Hift. Vol. XV. p. 363.
[z] Crevier, Rom. Emp. Vol. I. p. 215. [a] Id. Vol. VII. p. 65.

danger

danger at home.   At firſt, they were plain and rude
ſtructures, by no means remarkable for beauty or
ſtate: but in latter times, no expences were thought
too great, to render them in the higheſt manner
ſplendid and magnificent; nothing being more uſual
than to have the greateſt actions of the heroes, for
whom they were erected, curiouſly carved, or even
the whole proceſſion of the triumph cut out, on the
ſides of theſe arches.   Thoſe built by Romulus were
only of brick; and that of Camillus (part of which
is ſaid ſtill to ſubſiſt) of plain ſquare ſtone: but
thoſe of Cæſar, Druſus, Titus, Trajan, Gordian,
&c. were entirely of marble [b].

Their form was, at firſt, ſemi-circular, from whence
they probably took their name.   Afterwards, they
were built ſquare, with a ſpacious arched gate in the
middle, and ſmaller ones on each ſide.   Upon the
vaulted part of the middle gate, hung little winged
images, repreſenting victory, with crowns in their
hands, which, when they were let down, they put
upon the conqueror's head as he paſſed under in
triumph [c].

Antiquarians reckon thirty-ſix of theſe arches in ancient Rome.   Thoſe that are noticed in this plan, and
of which ſome parts yet remain tolerably perfect, are
the following:

Arcus Boarius, likewiſe called *Arcus Aurificum*,
(CD. *de*. 243), built by the merchants and bankers
of Rome, near the *Forum Boarium*, in honour of the
emperors M. Aurelius and L. Septimius Severus,
as an inſcription on it, ſtill extant, teſtifies.

Camillus's Arch (CD. *cd*. 150), ſuppoſed by ſome
to be one of Domitian's; and by others, with greater
probability, to have been erected in honour of
Druſus, ſon-in-law of Auguſtus, for his victories
over the Germans.   It is now called *l'Arco di*

[c] Fabricii, Roma. c. 14.   [b] Id. c. 15.

Portugal-

Portugallo [a], from the cardinal of Portugal, who once lived there.

Conftantine's Arch [b] (DE. *e.* 280), near the Colifeum; erected to Conftantine, by the fenate and Roman people, for his victory over Maxentius.

Gallienus's Arch [c] (D. *de.* 264), now called the arch of *St. Vitus*, near whofe church it ftands, was built, as the infcription denotes [d], by M. Aurelius, a private man, in honour of the emperor Gallienus.

We find alfo another arch of *Gallienus* in this plan, between the letters F and G, and over againft *e.*

Gordian's Arch (HI. *de*), by whom built, or upon what occafion, we know not; no mention being made of it, that we can find, in any of the writers who have defcribed ancient Rome.

Severus's Arch [e] (C. *cd.* 195), a magnificent fabric, erected by the fenate and Roman people, as the infcription on it teftifies [f], in honour of the emperor L. Septimius Severus. It is now confiderably funk in the earth. We have a fine drawing of this arch in Piranefi's *Views of Rome.*

Titus's Arch (DE. *de.* 281), erected, fome think, by the fenate and Roman people to Titus and his father Vefpafian, as a triumphal arch for their victories; but more probably dedicated to the memory of Titus, after his death, as Donatus [g] conjectures from the infcription ftill extant on this arch.

We do not here meet with one of that prodigious number of triumphal arches which Domitian erected to himfelf, as M. Crevier informs us [h].

---

[a] Nardini, & Donat. l. 3.
[b] Defcribed by M: Crevier, in the Xth vol. of his hiftory of the Roman Emperors, p. 67.
[c] See Crevier, Vol. IX. p. 107.
[d] Donat. l. 3. & Nardini, l. 4. c. 3.
[e] See Crevier, Vol. VIII. p. 115.
[f] Donat. l. 2.
[g] Lib. 3. p. 202 and 208.
[h] Vol. VI. p. 311, and 340.

BASILICÆ.

The *Basilicæ* of the Romans were very spacious and beautiful buildings, intended chiefly for the *Centumviri*, or judges, to sit in and hear causes, and for the counsellors to receive clients. The bankers too had one part of them allotted for their business[1]. Vossius has observed[k], that these *Basilicæ* were exactly in the shape of our churches; which was the reason that, upon the ruin of many of them, Christian churches were often raised on the old foundations : and hence too, perhaps, our great churches or cathedrals are still called *Basilicæ*.

Those noticed in this plan, are,

The *Basilic* and Portico of *Caius* and *Lucius Cæsars* (GH. *ef*); built by Augustus in honour of his nephews : and *Constantine's Basilica* (F. *f g*).

BATHS (THERMÆ).

There cannot well be a greater instance of the magnificence, or rather luxury, of the Romans, than their *Baths*. Ammianus Marcellinus says [1], they were built *in modum Provinciarum*, as large as provinces : to soften which exaggerated expression the learned Valesius [m] thinks we ought to read *Piscinarum*, instead of *Provinciarum*. Though this emendation may, perhaps, in some measure extenuate part of the vanity with which the Romans have been so often charged, in consequence of this passage of the historian ; yet the prodigious accounts we have of the ornaments and furniture of their baths, will bring them under a censure not less unfavourable than the former. Seneca, speaking of the luxury of his coun-

---

[1] Rosin. Antiq. l. 9. c 7.   [1] Lib. 16.
[k] In voce *Basilica*.   [m] Nota ad locum.

trymen

trymen in this refpect, complains, that they were arrived to fuch a pitch of nicenefs and delicacy, as to
fcorn to fet their feet on any thing but precious
ftones [n]; and Pliny wifhes, good old Fabricius were
but alive to fee the degeneracy of his pofterity, when
the very women muft have their feats in the baths,
of folid filver [o].

The moft remarkable of thefe *Baths*, of which
there ftill remain parts which fhew the vaft height of
their arches, the beauty of their pillars, the extraordinary quantity of foreign marble employed in
making them, the curious vaulting of their roofs,
and the number, ornaments, and conveniencies of
their fpacious apartments, are thofe of

Antoninus Caracalla (D. *fg*) [p].

Dioclefian (GH. *cd*): amazingly vaft and magnificent [q].

Titus Vefpafian (EF. *e*).

Others, likewife noticed in this plan, but lefs fpacious, are thofe of

Adrian (BC. *ab.* 18).

Agrippa (CD..*cd.* 146), fo named from the great
man who built them for the common ufe of all the
inhabitants of Rome [r]. The emperor Adrian rebuilt
them [s]. But being informed of the many abufes to
which the promifcuous admittance of men and women
gave rife, he forbad both fexes going to the fame baths [t]:
and Marcus Aurelius ordered that none of the public
baths fhould be opened before two o'clock in the af-
ternoon [u], except for fick people. The old practice
being renewed under the infamous reign of Helioga-

---

[n] Epift. 85.
[o] Lib. 33. c. 12.
[p] For the defcription of thefe baths, fee Crevier's Rom. Emp. Vol. VIII. p. 209.
[q] For a defcription of them, fee Crevier's Rom. Emp. Vol.

IX. p. 299.
[r] Crevier's Rom. Emperors, Vol. I. p. 55.
[s] Id. Vol. VII. p. 154.
[t] Id. ibid. p. 160.
[u] Ibid. p. 275.

balus,

balus, Alexander Severus again put a ſtop to it [w] :
and the emperor Tacitus ordered all public baths to
be ſhut by ſun-ſet [x].

Conſtantine (E. *cd*).

Decius (CD. *ef*). And CD. *f*. And again F. *de*.

Gordian (FG. *e*).

Nero, rebuilt by Adrian (CD. *bc*. 94).

Philip (G. *ef*).

Septimius Severus (B. *de*) together with his *Septi-zonium* [y] (DE. *ef*), which was alſo a bath, ſupported
by ſeven rows of pillars.

Trajan (EF. *de*).

BRIDGES.

There were formerly eight bridges over the Tiber,
the names of which, as enumerated by Martianus,
were, 1. *Sublicius*. 2. *Palatinus* or *Senatorius*. 3. *Fa-bricius*. 4. *Ceſtius*. 5. *Janiculenſis*. 6. *Triumphalis*.
7. *Ælius* ; and 8. *Milvius*. Of theſe, only five now
remain, *viz*. *Palatinus, Fabricius, Ceſtius, Janicu-lenſis*, and *Ælius*.

The bridge *Sublicius* (BC. *e*), the firſt bridge that
was built at Rome, was made by Ancus Martius,
intirely of oak ; whence Ovid calls it *roboreus*. It
was here that the brave Horatius Cocles kept at
bay the whole army of the Tuſcans commanded
by Porſena [z] : and from hence alſo the dead body of
Heliogabalus was thrown into the Tiber [a]. It crôſſed
the Tiber from the foot of mount Aventine, to
the ſpot here called *prata Mutia*, and led towards He-truria. A ſudden inundation broke down this bridge,
in lieu of which the prætor Emilius Lepidus built one

[w] Crevier's Roman Empe-rors, Vol. VIII. p. 289.

[x] Id. Vol. IX. p. 199.

[y] See Crevier, Vol. VIII. p.
134. and Montfaucon's Antiq.

Vol. V. p. 122.

[z] Rollin's Rom. Hiſt. Vol. I.
p. 228.

[a] Crevier's Rom. Emp. Vol.
VIII. p. 271.

of

of ftone : this alfo being deftroyed by the rifing of the water, the emperor Tiberius built another of ftone ; and this perifhing by the fame means, the emperor Antoninus Pius built a new one, of marble, and more lofty than the former. But this has alfo been demolifhed by the overflowing of the Tiber, and only fome few remains of it are now to be perceived, near the banks and under the water.

The bridge *Palatinus*, as it was formerly called, now *St. Mary's Bridge* (C. *de*), croffes over from the prefent church of St. Mary the Egyptian, at the lower end of the *Forum Boarium*, to the *via Tranftiberina*. This bridge is fuppofed to be that which Livy fpeaks of [a], built by M. Fulvius, wafhed down by the Tiber, and afterwards rebuilt by the cenfors Scipio Africanus and L. Mummius. Another inundation having damaged it, pope Gregory XIII. repaired it, partly upon the old piles, in the year 1575. But another inundation fweeping away fome of it in 1598, it has never fince been repaired, fo as to be ferviceable [b].

A little higher up the river, two very ancient bridges of ftone connect the ifland in the Tiber, formerly facred to Efculapuis, to whom a temple was built there [c], and now called St. Bartholomew's ifland, with the city on each fide of it. One of thefe, diftinguifhed by the name of *Fabricius*, (C. *d*), was built by the conful *Fabricius* when *Curator. Viarum*, in the year of Rome 692, as an infcription ftill remaining upon one of the piers, teftifies, and as Dion fays, *l*. 37. Another infcription on it witneffes it's having been repaired by the confuls Q. Lepidus and M. Lollius, which muft have been in the year of Rome 731. It is now called *Quattro capi*, from a fquare piece of marble that ftands at one end of it [d].

[a] Decad. 4. l. 10.
[b] Donat. l. 3.
[c] See Rollin's Roman Hiftory, Vol. III. p. 307.
[d] Denat. l. 3. & Nardini.

The

The bridge from the other fide of the ifland to the *Regio Tranftiberina* (C. *d*), was built by Cæftius, under the emperors Valentinian, Valens, and Gratian, as two infcriptions on it certify. It is ftill known by it's ancient name of *Ceftius*'s bridge, as well as by it's more modern one, of *St. Bartholomew*'s.

The bridge *Janiculenfis* (BC. *cd*), thought by Marlianus, and others, to have been built of marble by the emperor Antoninus (in which Nardini differs from them [f]), was alfo called anciently *Pons Aurelius*. It now bears the name of *Sixtus*, from pope Sxtus IV, who rebuilt it with great magnificence [g].

Some few ruins yet remain of the *Vatican Bridge* (BC. *b*), formerly called the *Triumphal*; not, fays Donatus, on account of the *Triumphal Gate*, which he will not allow to have ftood there: at the fame time declaring, that it is much eafier to fay where that gate did not ftand, than to point out where it did [h].

The bridge *Ælius* (C. *b*) was built by the emperor Ælius Adrian, and led to his tomb, now called the caftle of *St. Angelo*, which laft name has been alfo given to the bridge. Nardini [i] gives us a reprefentation of this bridge, as it was in ancient times, from the reverfe of a medal of the emperor Adrian.

The bridge *Milvius*, now called *Ponte Mole*, two miles beyond the *Porta Flaminia*, or prefent gate *del Popolo*, and confequently beyond the limits of this plan, was built by Emilius Scaurus, from whofe name the word *Milvius* has been formed by corruption [k]. It was repaired by pope Nicholas V, but only the foundations of it now remain.

Donatus [l], quoting Suetonius, fpeaks of a ninth bridge in Rome, built by Caligula, from the Palatine hill to the Capitol: and we find in Piranefi's

[f] Donat l. 8. c. 3.
[g] Donat. l. 3. p. 309. who quotes Eccl. Hift. l. 2. c. 12.
[h] Roma vetus ac recens, l. 1.
p. 78. & l. 3. p. 309.
[i] Roma Antica, l. 8. c. 3.
[k] Nardini, l. 8. c. 3.
[l] Lib. 2. p. 158.

Views

Views of Rome, a drawing of a fluted pillar, said to be one of those which supported this bridge.

CAMPI.

The ancient Romans diftinguifhed feveral fpaces of ground, or fields, by this name; but the moft famous by far, originally a large open field, lying near the *Tiber*, whence we find it fometimes called *Tiberinus*, was the

Campus Martius (CE. *ac.* 46), fo called, becaufe it was confecrated to the god *Mars*.

Befides it's pleafant fituation, and other natural ornaments, the continual exercifes and fports performed here, and the frequent affemblies of the people in ancient times, made this, particularly then, one of the moft remarkable places near the city; for here, as Kennet obferves, the young nobility practifed all manner of feats of activity, and learned the ufe of all forts of arms and weapons. In later days it was encompaffed with a wall, and nobly adorned with ftatues of famous men, arches, columns, porticos, and other magnificent ftructures. Here ftood the *Villa publica,* or palace for the reception and entertainment of ambaffadors from foreign ftates, who were not allowed to enter the city. Several of the public *Comitia* were held in this field; and for that purpofe the *Septa* (DE. *bc.* 54), or *Ovilia* as fome called them, a fpace where the Tribes or Centuries went in one by one to vote, were inclofed with rails. Cicero, in one of hisepiftles to Atticus, intimates a noble defign he had to make the *Septa* of marble, and to cover them with a high roof, with the addition of a ftately *Portico* or *Piazza* all round: but as we hear no more of this project, we may reafonably fuppofe that he was difappointed by the civil wars which broke out foon after [m].

* Kennet's Rom. Antiq.

We

We likewife find, in the annexed plan, the

Campus Efquilinus (H. *cd*), bordering upon the *Efquiline* hill, from whence it derived it's name.

Campus Judeorum, or *Jews Field* (B. *de*), which we take to be a modern appellation.

Campus Sanctus (F. *f*), likewife a modern name.

Campus Sceleratus (GH. *bc*. 296), or the *wicked Field*; fo called, according to Donatus [n], becaufe fuch of the veftals as broke their vow of chaftity, were buried there alive : and accordingly we find marked in the fame place, in this plan, the fpot where they were fo buried. But this, according to the above-mentioned author [o], muft be a miftake; a pofitive law of the Romans enacting, that no dead body whatever fhould be buried or burnt within the walls of the city : much lefs is it probable, as he obferves, that the ftate fhould fuffer capital convicts to be buried there alive. The place deftined for that dreadful execution feems rather to have been fomewhat farther, to the right, without the walls ; which would agree with Livy [p], who, fpeaking of the veftal Minucia, on whom this punifhment was inflicted, fays, fhe was buried alive in a field beyond the gate *Collina*, here called *Salaria*, (H. *bc*) [q].

The *Field of Tarquin the Proud*, or *Campus Tarquinii Superbi* (H. *d*).

CIRCI.

The *Circi* of the Romans were places fet apart for feveral forts of games, but particularly races. They were generally oblong [r], furrounded with a wall [s], and ranges of feats for the convenience of the fpectators. At the entrance of the *Circus* ftood the

---

[n] Lib. 3. p. 275.
[o] Loco fupr. citat.
[p] Decad. 1. l. 8.
[q] M. Rollin mentions her be-ing put to this death, in his

Rom. Hift. Vol. III. p. 132.
[r] Marlian. Topogr. Rom. Ant. l. 4. c. 10.
[s] Polydor. Virg. de Rer. in-vent. l. 2. c. 14.

Carceres,

Carceres, or Lifts, from whence the racers ftarted; and juft by them one of the *Metæ*, or goals. The other *Meta* ftood at the farther end, to conclude the race.

There were feveral of thefe *Circi* in Rome: but the principal one, as it's name imports, was the *Circus Maximus* (CD. *ef*), firft built by the elder Tarquin [t]. The length of it was 2205 feet, and it's breadth 950: and round it were as many feats, in rows one above the other, as would contain an hundred and fifty thoufand people [u]. Julius Cæfar adorned it with magnificent buildings, and fine canals of water, to reprefent fea-fights in them. Auguftus enlarged it, and erected in it an obelifc an hundred and fifty feet high. The emperor Claudius built dens, or *Carceres*, as they are called in this plan (CD. *de*. 300), of marble, inftead of thofe which had till then been made only of earth, or wood, for the wild beafts ufed in this Circus. Caracalla caufed divers parts of it to be painted and gilded; and Heliogabalus ordered it's floor to be ftrewed with gold and filver duft. Thefe emperors enlarged this *Circus* to fo vaft an extent, that they rendered it capable of holding two hundred and fixty thoufand fpectators, in their proper places [w].

The other *Circi* noticed in this plan, are,

Nero's Circus (AB. *ab*. 2), in the Vatican valley, within the gardens of that emperor, as Tacitus informs us [x]. The magnificent church of St. Peter now ftands on that very fpot [y]. The *Meta*, or goal of this *Circus* ftood, according to Nardini [z], precifely where the fine obelifc erected by pope Sixtus V. now is.

[t] Liv. & Dionyf. Halycarn. & Rollin, Rom. Hift. Vol. 1. p. 137.
[u] Dionyf. l. 3.
[w] Plin. l. 36.
[x] Annal. 14.
[y] Nardini, l. 7. c. 13.
[z] Ibid.

Circus

Circus Agonalis (CD. *bc*), now the *Piazza Navona*, finely drawn by Piranesi. Antiquarians are far from being agreed why this *Circus* was called *Agonalis.* That the Romans had an immoveable feast, instituted by their king Numa, which was celebrated every year on the 9th of January, in honour of the god *Janus*, as we learn from *Ovid* [a], is very certain. The *Rex sacrorum* at this feast sacrificed a wether to the god *Janus.* In consequence of this, Varro [b] derives the word *Agonalis* from a ceremony used in all sacrifices, where the priest, being ready to offer the sacrifice, asks the sacrificer, *Agon*', which was used then for *Agamne*, Shall I strike? Festus derives this word either from *Agonia*, which signifies a sacrifice, or from *Agonius*, the god of action, or from *Agones*, which signify mountains, and so the *Agonalia* were sacrifices which were offered upon a mountain. Indeed the *Quirinal* hill was called *Agonus*; and the gate *Collina*, which led thither, *Porta Agonensis*; which the same *Festus* will have to have been so called from the games which were celebrated without that gate in honour of Apollo, near the temple of *Venus Erycina*, when the *Circus Flaminius* was overflowed by the Tiber, as we shall have occasion to observe in speaking of the gate *Salaria.*—But it is more probable that the word *Agonalia* came from the Greek ἀγὼν, which signifies sports and combats, such as were used in Greece, in imitation of those first instituted by Hercules at Elis, and consecrated to Jupiter, as Ovid informs us [c].

The *Stadia* were places in the form of *Circi*, for the running of men and horses [d]. A very noble one, Suetonius tells us [e], was built by Domitian: but as it is not noticed in this plan, we presume there are no remains of it now subsisting.

[a] Fast. l. 1. v. 317.
[b] Lib. 5.
[c] Fast. l. 1. v. 359.
[d] Fabric. Rom. c. 12.
[e] In Domitiano.

COLUMNS

ANCIENT ROME.

COLUMNS and OBELISCS.

The pillars of the emperors *Trajan* and *Antoninus* deferve particular notice.

Trajan's Column[f] (DE. *cd.* 172), compofed of twenty-four great pieces of marble, fo nicely cemented as to feem to make but one ftone, was erected in the middle of that emperor's *Forum*. It's height, according to Eutropius[g], was 144 feet; though Marlian[h] feems to make them but 128. This difference may be reconciled, by fuppofing one of thefe writers to have given only the meafure of the pillar itfelf, and the other to have included the bafis. It is afcended on the infide by 185 winding fteps, and has 40 little windows for the admiffion of light. The whole pillar is incrufted with marble; on which are reprefented all Trajan's noble actions, and particularly the Dacian war. One may fee all over it figures of forts, bulwarks, bridges, fhips, &c. and all manner of arms, as fhields, helmets, targets, fwords, &c. together with the feveral offices and employments of the foldiers; fome digging trenches, fome meafuring out a place for the tents, and others making a triumphal proceffion[i]. But the nobleft ornament of this pillar was the ftatue of Trajan on the top, twenty two feet high, dreffed in his military robe, and holding in his left hand a fcepter, and in his right a hollow globe of gold, in which his afhes were repofited after his death[k].

Antoninus's Column (DE. *bc.*71), was erected by the emperor Marcus Aurelius and the fenate in honour of his predeceffor, Titus Antoninus, and in imitation of that of *Trajan,* which it exceeded only in this re-

[f] See Crevier, Vol. VII. p. 47. and 98.
[g] Hift. l. 9.
[h] Lib. 3. c. 13.
[i] Vide Crevier, Vol. VII. p. 98.
[k] Fabricius, c. 7.
[l] Cafalius, Par. 1. c. 11.

fpect,

spect, that it was 176 feet high[l]. The ascent, on the inside, was by 106 steps, and the windows in the sides were 56. The sculpture and other ornaments were of the same nature as those on Trajan's column; but greatly inferior in point of workmanship; being done in the declining age of the empire. On the top of this pillar stood a colossal statue of the emperor Antoninus, naked, as appears from some of his coins.

Both these columns are still standing at Rome; the former most intire. But pope Sixtus the first, instead of the two statues of the emperors, set up *St. Peter*'s on the column of *Trajan*, and *St. Paul*'s on that of *Antoninus*[m].

The famous *Columna miliaria* (D. *de*. 283), called also *Miliarium aureum*, was a gilded pillar, erected in the *Forum* by Augustus[n], as the point from whence all the high-ways of Italy were to be measured[o]. From this the Romans counted their miles, at the end of every one of which a stone was set up, marked with the distance from Rome.

Two *Antique Columns*, the particulars of which we know not, stand at D. *c*. 69, and between DE and *cd*. 152.

Between AB and *ab*, at *fig*. 4. is a fine Egyptian *Obelisc*, erected by pope Sixtus V. in the front of St. Peter's. At D*b*. 51. and D*c*. 88. are two other *Obeliscs*; and between GH and *bc* stands an *Obelisc* formerly dedicated to the moon. Some of these, but we cannot pretend to say which, were probably those M. Crevier mentions[p] being brought to Rome, from Egypt, by Caligula, at a vast expence.

[l] Marlian. l. 6. c. 13.
[m] Casal. Par. 1. c. 11.
[n] See Crevier, Vol. I. p. 1c4.
[o] Marlian. l. 3. c. 18.
[p] Vol. III. p. 74.

Thé DOMI,

Or Houfes, remarkable either for their fize, or former inhabitants, mentioned in this plan, are thofe of

Pompeius Atticus (EF. *cd.* 292), on the Quirinal hill.

The *Cornelii* (E. *cd.* 290), near Conftantine's baths.

The *Gordians* (H. *e*).

Licinius (GH. *e.*)

Martial (G. *bc*).

Pilate (C. *de.* 239).

The *Pincii* (EF. *bc.* 239).

Pompey the Great (GH. *e*).

Titus (FG. *ef*).

FORA.

The Roman *Fora* were commonly about three times as long as they were broad. The whole com-pafs of the *Forum* was furrounded with arched por-ticos, only fome paffages being left for places of en-trance. Their fituation was, generally, fo contrived, that fome of the moft ftately edifices, fuch as tem-ples, theatres, bafilicæ, &c. ftood round, or near them [s].

They were of two forts; *Fora Civilia* and *Fora Venalia*. The former were defigned for the ornaments of the city, and for the ufe of public courts of juftice: the others, like our markets, were intended for the convenience of the people.

Of the *Fora Civilia* there were five confiderable in Rome, *viz.*

[s] Lipfius, de Magnit. Rom.

Auguftus's

Auguſtus's Forum [r] (DE. *d.* 169), built by Auguſtus Cæſar, and reckoned by Pliny among the wonders
of the city.   The moſt remarkable curioſity was the
ſtatues in the two porticos on each ſide of the main
building.   In one, were all the Latin kings, beginning with Æneas ; in the other, all the kings of
Rome, beginning with Romulus ; moſt of the eminent
perſons in the commonwealth, and Auguſtus himſelf
among the reſt ; with an inſcription upon the pedeſ-
tal of every ſtatue, expreſſing the chief action and ex-
ploits of the perſon it repreſented [s].   This *Forum*
was reſtored by the emperor Adrian [t].

Cæſar's, or the *Julian Forum* (DE. *de.* 285), built by
Julius Cæſar, with the ſpoils taken in the Gallic war.
It's area alone, Suetonius tells us [u], coſt an hundred
thouſand ſeſterces ; and Dio [x] affirms it to have much
exceeded the Roman Forum.

Nerva's Forum (DE. *d.* 164), begun by Domitian [y],
but finiſhed and named by the emperor Nerva.   In
this *Forum* Alexander Severus ſet up the ſtatues of all
the emperors that had been deified [z], in imitation of
what Auguſts had done in his *Forum.* This *Ferum* was
called *Tranſitorium* [a], becauſe it lay very convenient
for a paſſage to the others ; and *Palladium,* from a
ſtatue of Minerva which was ſet up in it [b].   Scarce any
thing remains of this *Forum,* except an old decayed
arch, which the people, by a ſtrange corruption, in-
ſtead of Nerva's arch, call Noah's ark [c].

The *Roman Forum* (DE. *de*), which was only a
large open ſpace in Romulus's time, without buildings
or any other ornament.   Tullus Hoſtilius firſt in-
cloſed it ; the elder Tarquin adorned it with porticos ;

.. [r] See Crevier, Vol. I. p. 84.
[s] Lipſ. de Magn. Rom.
[t] Spartian. in Hadriano.
[u] In Jul. Cæſ. c. 26.
[x] Lib. 43.
[y] Suet in Domit. c. 5.

[z] Spartian. in Severo.
[a] Nardini, Roma Antica, l. 3.
c. 14. & Donat. l. 2. c. 23.
[b] Lipſ. de Magn. Rom.
[c] Marlian. l. 3. c. 14.

and fucceeding kings, confuls, and magiftrates, rendered it at length one of the nobleft places in the
world. It was called *Forum Romanum*, or fimply
Forum, by way of eminence, on account of it's anti-
quity, in comparifon of the other *Fora*, and of it's
moft general ufe in public affairs. Martial [a] and
Statius [e], for the fame reafon, give it the name of
Forum Latium ; Ovid the fame [f] ; and of *Forum Mag-
num* [g] ; and Herodian [b] calls it τὴν ἀρχαῖαν ἀγορὼν, *The
Old Forum*. Statius [i] has given an accurate defcription of this *Forum*, in his poem upon the equeftrian
ftatue of Domitian fet up there by that emperor : but
at the fame time antiquarians are fo divided about
it's exact extent, that it would be extremely difficult,
if not impoffible, now to afcertain that point. It's
fituation, we know, was between the Capitoline hill
and the Palatine, as marked in this plan.

The *Comitium*, ufed fometimes for holding the
Comitia, was a part of this *Forum*, in which ftood the
Roftra, a fort of pulpit, adorned with the beaks of
fhips taken in a fea-fight from the inhabitans of An-
tium [k]. In this, the caufes were pleaded, the ora-
tions made, and the panegyrics fpoken by perfons at
the death of their friends or relations.—Hard by
was the *Puteal*, of which critics give very different
accounts, but none more probable than the opinion
of the ingenious M. Dacier [l], according to whom,
the Romans, whenever the thunder fell upon a place
without a roof, took care, out of fuperftition, to have
a fort of cover built over it, which they called *Puteal*.
This had the name of *Puteal Libonus*, and *Scribonium
Puteal*, becaufe *Scribonius Libo* erected it by order
of the fenate. The prætor's tribunal, which ftood

[a] Epigr. l. 2.
[e] Sylvar. l. 1. c. 1.
[f] Faft. 4.
[g] Faft. 3.
[b] In vit. M. Antonin.

[i] Sylvar. l. 1. c. 1.
[k] Livy, & Fabricii Roma, c. 13.
[l] Notes on Horace, l. 2. Sat. 6. v. 35.

2   juft

juſt by, is often denoted by the ſame expreſſi-
on.

Trajan's Forum [m] (DE. *d.* 170), built by the emperor Trajan, with the produce of the ſpoils he had
taken in his wars. The porticos round this Forum
were exceedingly beautiful and magnificent, covered
with braſs, and ſupported by pillars of more than ordinary ſize, and exquiſite workmanſh ip.

Of the chief *Fora Venalia*, or markets, in ancient
Rome, which were, 1. The *Forum Boarium*, for
oxen and beef; 2. *Suarium*, for ſwine; 3. *Piſtorum*,
for bread; 4. *Cupedinarum*, for dainties; and 5.
Olitorium, for roots, ſallads, and ſuch like; we have
in this plan,

The *Forum Boarium*, between the letters CD and
de; and the

Forum Olitorium, between CD and *cd*, marked
182.

Beſides which we find five other *Fora*, viz. *Forum
Eſquilinum* (GH. *de*), upon mount *Eſquiline*.

Forum Nummulariorum, between BC and *bc*, marked
24, near the

Forum Pontis, under the letter C, and overagainſt
b, at the foot of the bridge Elius, now *St. Angelo.*

Forum Populi (DE. *a*), and the

Forum Salluſtii, between the letters CD and *de*,
denoted by the cyphers 295, and ſo called, probably, from the name of the perſon who built it.

GARDENS.

Of the many ſpacious gardens formerly in Rome
we find only the following noticed in this plan.

The *Cæſarean* gardens (B. *de*).

Thoſe of *Mecænas*, (H. *d*); and

Thoſe of *Salluſt* (FG. *bc*).

---

[m] See Crevier, Vol. VII. p. 47. and 99. [a] Marlian. l. 3. c. 13.

GATES.

ANCIENT ROME.

GATES.

Romulus built only three, or, as some will have it, at most four gates : but as the city was enlarged, the gates were multiplied, so that Pliny tells us, there were thirty-four in his time. There are now, as marked in the annexed plan, which agrees with the number reckoned by Procopius [n] in his time, four-teen, which we shall range in the following alphabetical order.

Asinaria, called also formerly *Cælimontana,* and *St. John's Gate* (FG. *fg*). Antiquarians differ greatly, and by no means determine whence came it's name of *Asinaria.* Donatus [o] thinks it may have been so called from a road of that name, to which it led ; or from gardens, called the *Asinarian,* situated near this gate ; or perhaps from Asinius Pollio, or Asinius Gallus, consuls under Augustus, who may have built or repaired it. Nardini leaves us equally in the dark. The name of *Cælimontana,* by which the ancients called it, was derived from it's situation upon *Mount Cælius.* But it's oldest name of all was *Querquetulana* [p]. Cicero mentions it by that name [q]. It is now called *St. John's Gate,* because it leads to *St. John Lateran.*

Aureliana (AB. *cd*), so called from the emperor *Aurelian,* who either rebuilt or repaired it. It is now named *St. Pancras's Gate,* from it's leading to the church of that saint. Some have called it *Trajana,* on account of it's having been repaired, say they, by the emperor Trajan : but it's first and oldest appellation was *Janiculensis ;* derived, probably, from the bridge of that name, which led to this gate [r].

[n] De Bello Goth. l. 1.
[o] Roma vetus ac recens, l. 1.
[p] Donat. l. 1.
[q] Ad Pison.
[r] Donat. & Nardini.

Capena

Capena (DE. *gb*): fo called from *Capua*, an old city of Italy, the way to which lay thro' this gate. It was alfo called *Appiana*, from it's leading to the *Appian Way*; and *Triumphalis*, from fome triumphs in which the proceffion paffed through it: though it does not feem to have been the gate appropriated to that cere-mony, the real fituation of which antiquarians are at a lofs to determine. The curious in thefe matters may confult Donatus, l. 1. c. 22. *De Portu Trium-phali.* The gate *Capena* was likewife called *Fontina-lis,* from the aqueducts which were raifed over it: whence Juvenal terms it *madida Capena,* and Martial, *Capena grandi Porta quæ pluit gutta.* It is now called *St. Sebaftian's Gate,* from a church dedicated to that faint, which ftands near it.

Efquilina (H. *e*), now the *Gate of St. Laurence,* to whofe magnificent church it leads. Antiquarians are not agreed, whether it was originally called *Efquilina,* from it's being built on mount *Efquiline*; or *Taurina,* from a head of an ox carved upon it; or *Tiburtina,* from it's leading to *Tibur,* now *Tivoli.* It feems alfo to have been anciently called *Libitinenfis,* on account of the dead bodies that ufed to be carried through it, in order to their being interred in the *Campus Efquilinus,* which was the general burying-place of the common people. Livy, Dionyfius, and Strabo, call it *Efquilina*; and the former of thefe authors (lib. 2.) fixes it's fituation, by faying, that it was directly overagainft the gate *Janiculenfis*; here called *Aureliana.*

Flaminia (DE. *a*), owing it's name to the *Flami-nian Way,* which begins there. Donatus fays [*] it was ftill more anciently called *Flumentana,* from it's prox-imity to the river Tiber. It is now called the Gate *del popolo,* from a church built near it by pope Paf-cal II, dedicated to the virgin Mary, under the ap-pellation of *Sancta Maria del Popolo.*

[*] Roma, l. 1. p. 66.

Gabiufa

Gabiufa (EF. *fg*), fo named formerly, according to Fulvius and Marlianus, from it's leading to a road called *Gabina*. St. Gregory[t] calls it *Metroni*, which name it ftill retains; but why we cannot fay. It is now walled up. This Gate, which is mentioned in Livy, was in the XIIIth ward, or region, of ancient Rome[u].

Latina, or *in via Latina* (EF. *gb*), fo called from it's leading to *Latium*, now the *Campagna di Roma*. It was alfo called Ferentina, from *Ferentinum*, a place upon the Latin way[x]. A chapel now ftands near it, dedicated to *St. John the Apoftle*, from whom the gate alfo is at prefent called.

Nævia (GH. *f*), now diftinguifhed by the name of *major*, or the *great Gate*, and alfo by that of *Sancti Crucis*, or the gate of the *Holy Crofs*, had it's appellation of *Nævia*, fays Varro, *à nemoribus*, from the woods which formerly ftood near it; or from an adjacent wood belonging to one *Nævius*. The Claudian aqueduct runs clofe by it. This gate was alfo called, formerly, *Præneftina* and *Labicana*; the roads to both thefe places lying through it.

Nomentana, now *St. Agnes* (H. *c*). The name *Nomentana*, or *Numentana*, was given this gate, becaufe it led to *Numentum*. It was likewife called *Viminalis*, on account of the ofiers that grew near it[y], or from it's fituation upon the defcent of mount *Viminalis*. It has alfo been called *Pia*, becaufe pope Pius IV. repaired it; and it's prefent name of *St. Agnes* is taken from the church of that faint, which ftands at fome diftance from it, without the walls.

Pinciana (FG. *b*), formerly called *Collatina*, becaufe it led to the town of that name in the country of the Sabines, not far from Rome[z].

---

[t] Lib. 9. ep. 38.
[u] Donat. l. 1.
[x] Strabo.

[y] Donat. l. 1. p. 68.
[z] Procop. de Bell. Goth. L. 1.

Portuenfis

Portuenfis (AB. *ef*), fo called, as well as the road it opens into, from their leading to the city formerly named *Portuenfis* ; now by corruption called *Villa Portefe*[a]. This gate, and the wall around it, were rebuilt by the emperors Honorius and Arcadius. It was alfo called *Navalis*, from its being near the river.

Salaria (H. *bc*), deriving it's name, as did alfo the road it leads to, from the falt which the Sabines ufed to bring into Rome that way from the fea. It was likewife called *Collina*, from it's ftanding juft at the junction of the hills *Quirinalis* and *Viminalis* ; and *Quirinalis*, from a chapel ,facred to Romulus (*Quirinus*), which ftood hard by ; and *Agonenfis*, on account of the games called *Agonalia*, which were celebrated juft without it, in honour of *Apollo*, as *Feftus* fays, (but of the god *Janus*, according to *Ovid*[b],) near the temple of Venus *Erycina* ; particularly when the Tiber rofe fo high as to overflow the *Circus Flaminius*.. It was through this gate[c] that the Gauls entered Rome, under the command of their leader Brennus, when that city was firft taken by them.

Septimiana (B. *cd*), from the emperor Septimius Serus[c], who built it, and whofe baths were juft without this gate. Pope Alexander VI. repaired it[d].

Trigemina (BC. *fg*), anciently fo named from the three Horatii, who went out at this gate to fight the three Curiatii. It has alfo been called *Appia*, from the *Appian* aqueduct which runs near it ; *Fontinalis*, from a number of fprings or fountains that are there ; and *Oftienfis*, on account of the road to *Oftium*, which begun there. It is now called the gate of *St. Paul*, from a noble church dedicated to that apoftle, to which it leads, without the walls, and of which

---

[a] Nardini.
[b] Faft. l. 1. v. 217.
[c] Procop. de Bell. Goth. l. 1.
[d] Donat. l. 1. p. 70.
[e] Nardini.

Piranesi has given us a most elegant drawing in his *Views of Rome*.

These were the principal gates of ancient Rome: besides which antiquarians mention several others; such as the gate *Carmentalis*, built by Romulus, and so called from *Carmenta* the prophetess, mother of Evander; the gates *Sangualis*, *Mutia*, *Catularia*, *Frumentaria*, *Stercoraria*, &c. but where they were situated, we know not; nor are any remains of them now to be seen.

In the wall which surrounds the space now occupied by St. Peter's church and the pope's palace (AC. *ab*), are the five following lesser gates, as marked in this plan, *viz.* the gate of the *Holy Ghost*, the gate *Posterula*, the gate *Fornacum*, the *Vatican* gate, and *St. Peter*'s gate.

HILLS.

The seven principal hills inclosed within the walls of ancient Rome, from whence the phrase of *Urbs septicollis*, and the like, so frequent with the poets, were *Mons Palatinus*, *Mons Capitolinus*, *Mons Quirinalis*, *Mons Cælius*, *Mons Esquilinus*, *Mons Viminalis*, and *Mons Aventinus*.

I. *Mons Palatinus.*—Whether the *Palatine* hill (D. *e*) received its name from a people called *Palantes* or *Palatini*; or from the bleating and strolling of cattle, in Latin *balare* and *palare*; or from *Pales*, the pastoral goddess; or from the burying-place of *Pallas*, is disputed by the learned, and undetermined [a]. Here Romulus laid the foundation of his city, in a quadrangular form, with the ceremonies described at length by M. Rollin, in his history of the Roman republic, *Vol. I. p. 17. & seq.* and here the same king

[a] For the origin of this name, see Rollin's Rom. Hist. Vol. I. p. 5.

and

and Tullus Hoſtilius kept their courts ; as did afterwards Auguſtus and all the ſucceeding emperors ;
on which account, the word *Palatium* came to ſigni-
fy a royal ſeat[b].   To the eaſt of this hill is *Mons Cælius* ; to the ſouth, *Mons Aventinus* ; to the weſt,
Mons Capitolinus ; and to the north, the *Forum*[c].   It's
compaſs is twelve hundred paces[d]. Romulus's houſe,
preſerved for ſeveral ages by the care of the ſenate,
was on this hill, near the ſpot where the church of *St.
Anaſtaſia* now ſtands ; as was alſo that of his foſter-
father *Fauſtulus*, near the place now occupied by the
church of *Sancta Maria Liberatrice.*

II. *Mons Capitolinus*, the *Capitoline* hill (CD. *d*), before named *Mons Tarpeius*, from *Tarpeia*, a Roman veſ-
tal, who betrayed the city to the Sabines in this place[e].
It was alſo called *Mons Saturni*, and *Saturnius*, in honour of *Saturn*, who is reported to have lived here in
his retirement, and was ever reputed the tutelar deity
of this part of the city. The name of *Capitolinus*
was afterwards given it from the head of a man
called *Tolus*, caſually found there in digging for
the foundations of the famous temple of Jupiter[f],
named, for the ſame reaſon, *Capitolium*. This
hill was added to the city by Titus Tatius, king of
the Sabines, when, having been firſt overcome in
the field by Romulus, he and his ſubjects were
permitted to incorporate with the Romans[g]. It has
to the eaſt, *Mons Palatinus* and the *Forum* ; to the
ſouth, the *Tiber* ; to the weſt, the level part of the
city ; and to the north, *Collis Quirinalis*[h]. It's compaſs was ſeven *ſtadia*, or furlongs[i]. This hill was the
moſt conſiderable of any in Rome, on account, particularly, of the buildings that ſtood upon it, which

[b] Roſin. Antiq. l. 1. c. 4.   Vol. I. p. 46.
[c] Fabricii Roma, c. 3.   [f] Liv. l. 1. c. 55.
[d] Marlian. Topograph. An-   [g] Dionyſius.
tiq. Roma, l. 1. c. 14.   [h] Fabricii Roma, c. 3.
[e] Plut. in Romul. See alſo   [i] Marlian. lib. 1. c. 1.
Rollin's Hiſt. of the Republ.

were

were a fortrefs and fixty temples, the moft confiderable of which, called the *Capitol*, we fhall take fur-
ther notice of when we come to fpeak of the buildings and temples of Rome.

III. *Mons Quirinalis*, the *Quirinal* hill, (F. *cd*), fo
called, either from the temple of *Quirinus*, another
name of Romulus; or, more probably, from the
Curetes, a people that removed thither with Tatius,
from *Cures*, a Sabine city [k]. It afterwards changed
it's name to *Caballus*, *Mons Caballi*, and *Caballinus*,
from the two marble horfes, with each a man holding
him, which are fet up there. They are ftill ftanding;
and, if the infcription on the pilafters be true, were
the work of Phideas and Praxiteles [l]; made by thofe
famous mafters to reprefent Alexander the Great, and
his Bucephalus, and fent to Nero, as a prefent, by
Tiridates, king of Armenia. This hill, which was
added to the city by Numa [m], has, to the eaft, *Mons
Efquilinus* and *Mons Viminalis*; to the fouth, the *Fora*
of Cæfar and Nerva; to the weft, the level part of
the city; to the north, *Collis Hortulorum*, now called
Pincius, and the *Campus Martius* [n]; and is almoft
three miles in circumference [o].

IV. *Mons Cœlius* (E. *fg*), owes it's name to Cœlius,
or Cœles, a famous Tufcan general, who pitched his
tents there, when he came to the affiftance of Romulus againft the Sabines [p]. Livy [q] and Dionyfius Halicarnaffenfis [r] attribute the taking of it in to Tullus
Hoftilius; but Strabo [s], to Ancus Martius. The other
names by which it was fometimes known, were *Quer-
culanus*, or *Quercitulanus*, and *Auguftus*: the firft oc-
cafioned by the abundance of oaks growing there; the
other impofed by the emperor Tiberius, when he had

[k] Sixt. Pomp. Feftus.
[l] Fabricii Roma, c. 3.
[m] Dionyf. Halic. lib. 2.
[n] Fabricii Roma, c. 3.
[o] Marlian. l. 1. c. 1.
[p] Varro de Ling. Lat. lib. 4.
[q] Lib. 1. c. 30.
[r] Lib. 3.
[s] Geogr. l. 5.

C 2 raifed

raised new buildings upon it after a fire [t]. One part
of this hill (EF. *f*) was called *Cæliolus* [u] and *Minor
Cælius*. To the east, it has the city-walls; to the
south, *Mons Aventinus*; to the west, *Mons Palatinus*;
to the north, *Mons Esquilinus* [w]. Its compass is
about two miles and a half [x].

V. The *Esquiline Mount* (FG. *df*) was anciently
called *Crispius* and *Oppius* [y]. The name of *Esquilinus*
was varied, for the easier pronunciation, from *Exqui-
linus*, a corruption of *Excubinus*, *ab Excubiis*, from
the watch that Romulus kept in this place [z]. It was
taken in by Servius Tullius [a], who had his royal seat
upon this hill [b]. Varro will have the *Esquiliæ* to be
properly two hills [c]; which opinion has been since
approved of by a curious observer [d]. To the east, it
has the city-walls; to the south, the *Via Labicana*;
to the west, the valley lying between *Mons Cælius* and
Mons Palatinus; to the north, *Mons Viminalis* [e]; and
is in compass about four miles [f].

VI. *Mons Viminalis* (FG. *cd*), derives its name
from the great quantities of osiers (*Vimina*) that grew
there. This hill, which has to the east the *Campus
Esquinalis*; to the south, part of the *Suburra* and the
Forum; to the west, *Mons Quirinalis*; and to the
north, the *Vallis Quirinalis* [g]; is in compass two miles
and a half [h], and was taken in by Servius Tullius [i].

VII. The name of *Mons Aventinus* (CE. *eg*) has oc-
casioned much dispute among the critics, some deriving the word from *Aventinus*, an Alban king [k]; some

[t] Tacit. Annal. 4. Suet. in
Tib. c. 48.
[u] Fabricii Roma, c. 3.
[w] Ibid.
[x] Marlian. l. 1. c. 1.
[y] Fabricii Roma, c. 3.
[z] Propert. lib. 2. Eleg. 4.
[a] Liv. l. 1. c. 44.
[b] Ibid.

[c] De Ling. Lat. l. 4.
[d] Marlian. l. 1. c. 1.
[e] Fabricii Roma, c. 3.
[f] Marlian. l. 1. c. 1.
[g] Fabricii Roma, c. 3.
[h] Marlian. l. 1. c. 1.
[i] Dionys. Halic. lib. 4.
[k] Varro de Ling. Lat. l. 4.

from

from the river *Avens*[k]; and others *ab Avibus*, from the birds which ufed to fly thither in great flocks from the Tiber[l]. It was likewife called *Murtius*, from *Murcia*, the goddefs of fleep, who had there a *Sacellum*, or little temple[m] : *Collis Dianæ*, from the temple of Diana[n] ; and *Remonius* from Remus, who would have the city begun in this place, and was buried here[o]: A. Gellius affirms[p], that this hill, being all along reputed facred, was never inclofed within the bounds of the city till the time of Claudius. But Eutropius[q] exprefsly attributes the taking of it in to Ancus Martius ; and an old epigram, inferted by Cufpinian, in his comment on Caffiodorus, confirms the fame.

To the eaft, it has the city-wall ; to the fouth, the *Campus Figulinus* ; to the weft, the Tiber ; and to the north, *Mons Palatinus*[r]. It's circuit is eighteen *ftadia*, or two miles and a quarter[s].

Befides thefe feyen principal hills, three others of inferior note were taken in, in later times, *viz.*

Collis Hortulorum, or *Hortorum* (EG. *ac*), which had it's name from the famous gardens of Salluft adjoining to it[t], and was afterwards called *Pincius*, from the *Pincii*, a noble family who had their feat there[u]. It has to the eaft and fouth, the plaineft part of *Mons Quirinalis* ; to the weft, the *Vallis Martia* ; and to the north, the walls of the city[w]. It's compafs is about eighteen *ftadia*[x]; and it was firft inclofed within the city-walls by the emperor Aurelian[y].

[k] Varro de Lingua Latin. lib. 4.
[l] Ibid.
[m] Sext. Pomp. Feftus.
[n] Martial.
[o] Plut. in Romul.
[p] Lib. 13. c. 14.
[q] Lib. 1.

[r] Fabricii Roma, c. 3.
[s] Marlian. l. 1. c. 1.
[t] Rofin. lib. 1. c. 11.
[u] Ibid.
[w] Fabricii Roma, c. 3.
[x] Marlian. lib. 1. c. 1.
[y] Rofin. lib. 1. c. 11.

Janiculus, or *Janicularis* (AC. *bd*), fo called either from an old town of the fame name, faid to have been built by Janus ; or, becaufe Janus dwelt and was buried there[z] ; or, becaufe it was a fort of *gate (Janua)* to the Romans, whence they iffued out upon the Tufcans[a]. The fparkling fands have at prefent given it the name of *Mons Aureus*, and by corruption *Montorius*[b] Two juft obfervations concerning this hill occur from an epigram of Martial. That it is the fitteft place to take one's ftanding for a full profpect of the city ; and that it is lefs inhabited than the other parts, by reafon of the groffnefs of the air[c]. It is ftill famous for the fepulchres of Numa, and the poet Statius[d]. To the eaft and fouth, it has the Tiber ; to the weft, the fields ; to the north, the Vatican[e]: and fo much of it as ftands within the city-walls is about five *ftadia* in circuit[f].

Mons Vaticanus (B. *a*), which owes its name to the anfwers of the *Vates*, or prophets, that ufed to be given there ; or to the god *Vaticanus* or *Vagitanus*[g]. It feems not to have been inclofed within the walls until the time of Aurelian.

This hill was formerly famous for the fepulchre of Scipio Africanus; fome remains of which are ftill, to be feen[h]. But it is more celebrated at prefent on account of St. Peter's church, the pope's palace, and the nobleft library in the world.

To the eaft it has the *Campus Vaticanus*, and the river ; to the fouth the *Janiculum* ; to the weft, the *Campus Figulinus*, or potter's field : to the north, the *Prata Quintia*[i]. It lies in the fhape of a bow drawn

[z] Rofin. l. 1. c. 11.
[a] Feftus.
[b] Fabricii Roma, c. 3.
[c] Martial. Epig. lib. 4. Ep. 64.
[d] Fabricii Roma, l. 1. c. 3.

[e] Fabricii Roma, l. 1. c. 3.
[f] Marlian. l. 1. c. 1.
[g] Feftus.
[h] Warcup's Hift. of Italy, Book 2.
[i] Fabricii Roma, c. 3.

up

up very high; the convex part ftretching almoft a mile [k].

Five other leffer hills, noticed in this plan, but of a more modern appellation, are,

Mons Albanus (CD. *bc.* 100).

Mons Citatorius (D. *bc*), or, as Donatus [l] and Nardini [m] call it, *Mons Citorius*, fo named, according to the former [n], who quotes Livy [o], from it's being the place where the centuries of the people were fummoned.

Mons Jordanus (C. *bc*), evidently a modern name.

Mons Pincius, as it is now called, formerly *Collis Hortulorum* (EH. *ab*).

Mons Teftaceus (B. *f*), a hillock, formed almoft intirely of potfherds and pieces of urns and other vafes: but how they came to be heaped up here in fuch quantities, antiquarians are at a lofs to fay. Some think it was the place where the urns were made of old for burying the afhes of the dead: but this does not fatisfy Donatus [p].

The greateft extent of the whole city was in the time of the emperor Valerian, who enlarged it's walls to fuch a degree, as to furround the fpace of fifty miles [q]. At prefent, the compafs of Rome is not above thirteen miles [r].

The number of it's inhabitants, in it's flourifhing ftate, Lipfius computes at four millions [s].

L U C I,
Confecrated Groves and Woods.

The fuperftition of confecrating groves and woods to particular deities, was a practice very ufual with

[k] Marlian. l. 1. c. 1.
[l] Lib. 3. p. 277.
[m] Lib. 6. c. 5.
[n] Lib. 4. p. 402.
[p] Dec. 3. l. 6.

[p] Roma Vet. ac recens, p. 252.
[q] Vopifc. in Aurelian.
[r] Fabricii Roma, c. 2.
[s] De magnitud. Rom.

the

the anciehts: for. not to 'fpeak' of thofe mentioned
in the holy fcripture,. Pliny tells us, that trees, in old
time, ferved for the temples of the gods. Tacitus
reports this cuftom of the old Germans; Q. Curtius,
of the Indians; and almoft all writers, of the Druids.
The Romans too were great admirers of this worfhip,
and therefore had their *Luci*, or *confecrated groves* in
moft parts of the city.

The moft probable reafon that can be given for
this practice, is, as the judicious Kennet very properly obferves in his Antiquities of Rome, taken from
the common opinion, that fear was the main principle
of devotion among the ignorant heathens: and therefore fuch dark and lonely feats, ftriking them with a
fudden dread, made them fancy, that fomething di-
vine muft refide in thofe places, which could produce in them fuch an awe and reverence at their entrance.

The confecrated groves and woods noticed in this
plan, were facred to

The prophetefs *Carmenta*, mother of Evander (C.e,
304)..

The goddefs *Hibernia* (C. e. 305),

Honour and *Virtue* (DE. gb).

Jupiter (CD. ef).

Mars and *Auguftus* (FG. de).

Mars and *Juno Lucina* (EF. de).

The *Mufes*; to whom was alfo erected a temple, indicated here by the words *Lucus & Templ. Camænarum*
(DE. gb).

Befides which, we find a grove defignated by the
proper name of

Lucus Æliorum (FG. e), belonging, probably, to
fome of the Ælian family; and another by that of

Lucus Efquilinus (GH. ef); fo called from the *Efquiline Hill*, on the declivity of which it ftood.

PALACES,

PALACES.

Thofe noticed in this plan, are,
The *Cæfarean* palace (DE. *cd.* 144),
Conftantine's palace (F. *fg*).
Dioclefian's palace (FG. *cd*).
Nerva's palace (DE. *de.* 165).

PORTICOS,

The *Porticos* of the Romans were magnificent ftructures, moft commonly annexed to public edifices, facred and civil, as well for ornament as ufe, and generally named either from fome temple that ftood near them, or from their authors, or from the nature and form of the buildings, or from the kind of fhops that were kept in them, or from fome remarkable painting in them, or from the places to which they joined [a].

These *Porticos* were fometimes put to very ferious ufes, fuch as even affemblies of the fenate, upon certain occafions; though they were principally intended for the pleafure of walking and riding in them; in the fhade in fummer, and in the dry in winter. Velleius Paterculus [b] mentions them as an inftance of the extravagant luxury of the Romans, when their manners grew more and more corrupt, after the otherwife happy conclufion of the Carthaginian war: and Juvenal [c] has a complaint to the fame purpofe.

The *Porticos* noticed in this plan, are,

That which Auguftus built in memory of his nephews *Caius* and *Lucius Cæfars* (GH. *ef*), and that of

The temple of *Quirinus* (EF. *cd*).

There were feveral others very famous in ancient Rome; but we do not find them mentioned here.

---

[a] Fabricii Roma, c. 13.   [c] Sat. 7.
[b] Lib. 2. c. 1.

STREETS.

DESCRIPTION OF

STREETS in ROME, and ROADS which entered that City.

It would be impoffible for us, now-a-days, to try to point out either all the ftreets of ancient Rome, or all the ways that lead to or from that capital of the world. We fhall therefore content ourfelves with ranging in their alphabetical order, thofe only which are noticed in this plan, *viz.*

Via Alexandrina (BC. *ab*), over the *Vatican* hill.

Alta Semita, the way from the Capitol to the gate *Nomentana*, now *St. Agnes*.

Appia (DE. *fg*), fo named from the cenfor *Appius Claudius*, who paved it.

Campania (FG. *gb*), fo called from its leading to *Campania*.

Campi Floræ (BC. *c*), leading to the *Campus Floræ*.

Capitolii & Templ. Apollinis (CD. *d.* 258).

Capitolina (CD. *cd*), from the *Capitol* to the *Forum Olitorium*, or Herb-market.

Cælimontana (FG. *fg*), the ftreet or road over mount *Cælius*.

Collatina (F. *bc*), leading to the gate *Collatina*, now *Pinciana*.

Gabiufa (EF. *fg*), which led from the gate *Gabiufa*.

Julia (BC. *bc*), fo named from Auguftus's daughter *Julia*.

Sub Janiculo (BC. *bc*), leading from the bridge *Janiculenfis*, on the other fide of the Tiber, to *Mons Vaticanus*.

Labiana (H. *fg*), leading into the country from the gate *Nævia*, now the gate of the *Holy Crofs*.

Lata (DE. *ab*. &c.), fo called from it's extent.

Longobarda (DE. *b*), near *Auguftus's Maufoleum*.

Nomentana, called alfo *Viminalis* (HI. *cd*), which led from the gate formerly called *Nomentana*, now *St. Agnes*.

Ofticnfis

Ostiensis (BC. *fg*), which led from Rome to *Ostium*, through the gate *Trigemina*, now *St. Paul'* gate.

Portuensis (AB. *ef*), leading from the gate of that name.

Posterula (AB. *ab*), leading from the gate *Posterula*.

Prænestina (HI. *fg*), the *Prænestini* road, through the gate *Nævia*.

Regulæ (BC. *cd*), so called, perhaps, from the famous *Regulus*.

Sacra (DE. *cd*), leading from the *Forum* to the place afterwards occupied by Conftantine's arch.

Salaria, called alfo *Collatina*, and *Quirinalis* (H. *ac*), led from the gate *Salaria*, which had alfo the names of *Collina* and *Quirinalis*.

Taurina (HI. *ef*), from the *Efquiline* gate.

Tiburtina (HI. *ef*), the road to *Tibur*, through the *Efquiline* gate.

Tranftiberina (BC. *de*), the road on the other fide of the Tiber, from the *Palatine* bridge.

TEMPLES.

The temples of the ancients were built after different manners : one fort was called *Antes* or *Paraftates*, becaufe there were no pillars or pediments, but only fquare pilafters, called *Antes*. Vitruvius gives us a model of this kind, in a temple of Fortune, the particulars of which are not known. A fecond kind of temple was called *Proftilus*, becaufe it had no pillars, but in the front : fuch was the temple of Ceres Eleufinà begun by Jetinus, and finifhed by Philo. A third fort of temple was called *Amphiproftylus*, that is, a double *Proftylus*, having columns behind, as well as before : fuch was the temple of Concord. A fourth was called *Periptere*, becaufe it had pillars all around ; and of this kind was the temple built to Honour and Virtue by the architect Mutius. A fifth fort of tem-

3   ple

ple was named *Pfeudo-Dipterus*, that is, a falfe *Dip-terus*, becaufe it had not the two rows of pillars which the *Dipterus* has; and of this kind was the temple of Diana in the city of Magnefia, built by Hermogenes Alabandinus. A fixth was called *Dipterus*, becaufe it was furrounded with two rows of pillars : of this fort was the temple of Diana at Ephefus, built by Ctefiphon and Metagenes. And a feventh fort, called *Hypethrum*, was open at top to the air and weather : fuch was the temple of Jupiter Olympus built at Athens, by Cof-futius, a Roman architect.

The following are the temples noticed in this plan.

Templum Antonini & Fauftinæ, the temple of *Anto-ninus* and *Fauftina* (D. *de.* 284), erected by the empe-ror Marcus Aurelius, in honour of his father-in-law, and predeceffor, *Titus Antoninus*, and of his wife *Fauftina* ; the behaviour of which laft little intitled her to any fuch diftinction [w]. Some confiderable re-mains of this temple ftill fubfift, and are the fubject of one of Piranefi's beautiful drawings.

Templum Apollinis, the temple of *Apollo* (CD. *de.* 270), built by Auguftus, in honour of his favourite deity, *Apollo*, after his victory at Actium, upon mount *Palatine* ; whence this temple was called that of *Apollo Palatinus* [x]. This ftructure, according to the accounts of ancient writers, was amazingly magnificent. It was built of the fineft marble of Claros, and embel-lifhed with the richeft ornaments, both within and without. It's gates were of ivory, enriched with *baffo-relievos*, reprefenting the *Gauls*, when they were thrown headlong down from the top of the Capitol, by T. Manlius [y]. In the frontifpiece was a chariot of the fun, of maffy gold, crowned with rays fo pro-digioufly refplendent, that they dazzled the eyes of

[w] See Crevier, Vol. VII. p. in his Rom. Hift. Vol. XV. p. 202 and 329.   315.
[x] See M. Rollin's account of   [y] Id. Vol. II. p. 313. the building of this temple, &c.

the

the beholders. Within the temple was a marble statue of *Apollo*, made by the celebrated *Scopas*; and a
coloffal one, of brafs, fifty feet high; together with
a candleftick, in the form of a tree, whofe branches
were covered with clufters of lamps, in imitation of
fruit. Upon thefe branches the poets ufed to hang
their poems which they offered up to *Apollo*, as Horace informs us [z]. To this temple, dedicated to the
god of arts, was, very properly, joined a noble library [a], filled with all the beft Greek and Latin authors then extant: and all around were fpacious porticos, for the ufe and convenience of the public.

Between DE and *gh* we find *Ara Apollinis*, an
altar dedicated to the fame god; juft without the
walls of Rome, upon the borders of mount Aventine.

Templum Augufti, the temple of *Auguftus* (D. *de*.
282), near the *Ruminal Fig-tree*; which laft has been
fpoken of already under the article ÆDES [b].

Templum Augufti & Bacchi, the temple of *Auguftus* and *Bacchus* (D. *de*. 277), near the *Forum*. How
thefe two came to be joined together in the dedication
of this temple, is more than we can tell.

Templum Bacchi, the temple of *Bacchus* (I. *bc*), without the walls of Rome. This temple, now the
church of *St. Conftantia* [c], is fupported on the infide
by twenty-four noble pillars of granite. It's ancient
mofaic cieling, and the old windows, by which the
light was let in from the roof, ftill remain. Behind
the prefent altar ftands an antique urn of porphery, all
of one piece, eight feet long, four and a half deep, and
five feet wide; it's cover upwards of two feet thick:
and on each fide of the altar, is an antique candleftick
of marble, finely wrought.

[z] Ep. 3. l. 1.
[a] See Rollin's Rom. Hift.
Vol. XV. p. 315.
[b] For the deification of Auguftus, and the building of this
temple to him, by order of the
fenate, fee Crevier's Rom. Emp.
Vol. III. p. 13 and 14.
[c] Of the infide of which Piranefi has given us a fine drawing.

Templum

Templum Bonæ Deæ, the temple of the goddefs *Bona*, or the *Good Goddefs* (BC. *ef.* 307). This deity, called alfo by the ancients *Fatua*, and *Senta*, was *Dry-as* the wife of *Faunus*, remarkable for her exemplary chaftity. The Roman ladies, who held her in great veneration, facrificed to her in the night, in a little chapel, into which men were not permitted to enter; nor were they allowed ever to be prefent at her facri-fices. It was for violating this rule, that Cicero pro-fecuted the debauched *Clodius* [a], who had found means to introduce himfelf into this chapel in difguife, and thereby polluted the myfteries of the good goddefs. —A folemn facrifice to her was celebrated yearly in the houfe of the high-prieft, who, though the chief minifter on all other fimilar occafions, was, on this, (becaufe of his being a man) obliged to quit his dwelling the moment the ceremonies began, and leave the performance of them to his wife, and the virgins confecrated to this goddefs, who were alfo affifted by the veftals. The place where this goddefs was facri-ficed to, was adorned with all forts of plants, except *myrtle*, which was forbidden, on account of it's being facred to *Venus*.

Templum & Lucus Camænarum, the temple and grove of the *Mufes* (DE. *gh*). When, or by whom, the former was built, and the latter dedicated, we know not.

Templum Cereris, the temple of *Ceres* (CD. *ef*), near the *Circus Maximus*. The *Cerealia* and *Ludi Ce-reales*, *Feafts* and *Plays* in honour of Ceres, were firft inftituted among the Romans by the edile *Memmius*, as appears from a medal on which is the effigies of *Ceres* holding in one hand three ears of corn, and in the other a torch, and having her left foot upon a ferpent, with this infcription, *Memmius Ædilis Cerea-lia primus fecit.* The Athenians had long before kept

[a] See Rollin's Rom. Hift. Vol. XII. p. 20—27.

a feaft

a feaft to her, which they called *Thefmophoria*, and *Eleufia*. The epithet of *Eleufina* was given to *Ceres* upon this ocafion. Searching all places for her daughter Proferpine, fhe came to *Eleufina*, where fhe undertook to be nurfe to *Triptolemus*, the fon of king *Eleufius*; and when he was grown up, fhe taught him the art of fowing corn and making bread. In return for fo great a benefit, he appointed her a feaft, and priefts, called *Eumolpides*, from his fon *Eumolpus*. Crowns of flowers were not ufed in this feaft, but of myrtle and ivy, becaufe Proferpine was ftolen while fhe was gathering flowers. Her votaries carried lighted torches, and ran about calling aloud for *Proferpine*, as fhe had done when in fearch of her upon mount *Ida*. The priefts of this goddefs were called *Taciti Myftæ*, becaufe they were not allowed to difcover their myfterious rites. The *Ifis* of the Egyptians was certainly the *Ceres* of the Romans.

Templum Claudii Cæfaris, the temple of *Claudius Cæfar* (EF. *fg*), whofe deification was propofed by Nero, and ordered by the fenate[e]. This temple was begun by Agrippina, and finifhed by Vefpafian.

Templum Concordiæ, the temple of *Concord* (CD. *d.* 254), and again (CD. *de.* 266). One of thefe was probably the temple which Tiberius dedicated to *Concord*, by order of his mother *Livia*[f].

Templum Dianæ, the temple of *Diana* (C. *f*). The firft temple built to this goddefs, at Rome, was on mount Aventine, in the reign of Servius Tullius, at the joint expence of the Romans and Latins, as a place for them to meet at yearly, to offer a facrifice, in commemoration of the league made between the two nations[g].

Templum Famæ, the temple of *Fame* (CD. *de.* 235). We know not by whom this temple was built, or when.

[e] See Crevier, Vol. IV. p. 4. [g] Rollin's Rom. Hift. Vol. I.
[f] Id. Vol. I. p. 269. p. 164.

Templum

Templum & Domus Familiæ Flavianæ, the temple and houfe of the *Flavian* family (FG. *cd*). This temple was built, and a college of priefts inftituted, in honour of the Flavian family, by the emperor Domitian [h].

Templum Fauni, the temple of *Faunus* (EF. *ef*). *Faunus* was king of the Aborigines, in Latium, at the time when Evander arrived there. Dionyfius of Halicarnaffus calls him the fon of Mars; and fays, that the Romans, after his death, made him one of the tutelar gods of the country; to which he adds, that, in procefs of time, it became a common opinion, that *Faunus* was the wild-god, whofe voice was heard by night in forefts, and frightened people. In effect, *Faunus* and *Pan* feem often to be confounded together, as the god of *Fear*. Ovid feems not to make any diftinction between them; and Aurelius Victor thinks, they were one and the fame. Virgil makes *Faunus* a god of oracles and predictions. From this *Faunus* were fuppofed to be derived the *Satyrs*, *Pans*, and *Sylvans*, formerly taken for *Genii* and demi-gods, inhabiting woods and mountains, and reprefented with fmall horns on their head, pointed ears, and the reft of their bodies like goats. The country-people worfhipped them, and offered them goats in facrifice. Thefe demi-gods were known to the Latins only, and not to the Greeks.

Templum Febris, T. Trajanorum, & T. Neptuni, the temple of *Fever*, of *Trajan*, and of *Neptune* (CD. *e*. 272), near the *Circus Maximus*. That the Romans built temples to mifchievous beings, for the fame reafon, we fuppofe, as the Indians now worfhip the devil, is very certain. But how the fame building comes here to be confecrated to *Fever*, *Trajan*, or the *Trajans*, and *Neptune*, is more than we can fay.

Templum Felicitatis, the temple of *Happinefs* (G. *de*). We find a temple of *Happinefs* mentioned by

[h] See Crevier, Vol. VI. p. 312.

Pliny,

Pliny[i], which probably was this; concerning which antiquarians tell us nothing farther, than that it was adorned with a ftatue of the goddefs, made by a famous ftatuary called Archecilas, which coft Lucullus fixty great feſterces.

Templum Fidei, the temple of *Faith* (CD. *de.* 274). Numa is faid [k] to have been the firſt that erected a temple and appointed public worſhip to *Fides*, *Faith*; and to have taught the Romans, that the moſt ſacred oath they could take, was to fwear *ex fide*, by their *faith*, or *veracity*. His intention was to render their promiſes, without writings or witneſſes, as firm and certain as contracts made and fworn to with the greateft formalities; and in this he fucceeded to his wifh. Polybius gives [l] this glorious teſtimony of the Romans, that they inviolably kept their *faith*, that is, their word, without any occaſion for witneſſes or ſecurities; whereas nothing could bind the Greeks to their promiſes.

Templum Fidei, T. Jovis Cuſtodis, the temple of *Faith*, and the temple of *Jupiter the Preſerver* (CD. *de.* 262). We have juſt fpoken of the former of thefe deities; and ſhall mention the latter, to whom alone we ſhall find another temple erected, under the word *Jupiter Cuſtos*. How they came to be joined here, is more than we can ſay.

Templum Floræ, the temple of *Flora* (CD. *ef*), near the *Circus Maximus*; and another, between GH, and *bc*, towards the Gate *Salaria*.—Varro reckons *Flora* among the divinities that were honoured by the Sabines, and introduced at Rome, when that people, with their king Tatius, joined themfelves to the Romans. Lactantius defcribes her as a courtezan, who left her fubſtance to the Roman people; in return for which they decreed her extraordinary honours, and games

[i] Lib. 36. c. 5.   [l] l. 1. p. 134. Plut. in Num.
[k] Liv. l. 1. c. 21. Dionyf.   [l] Lib. 6.

D   called

called *Floralia*, where fhe was intitled the goddefs of flowers. Thefe games were firft inftituted five hundred and thirteen years after the foundation of Rome. We do not find that they were kept annually : but in the year five hundred and eighty, at the celebrating of them, harlots dancpd naked, with a thoufand lafcivious tricks and poftures. We find the place where they danced thus marked in this plan, between the temple we are fpeaking of, and the Salarian way, with the words *Ludi Florales meretricium nudarum.*

Templum Malæ Fortunæ, the temple of *Bad Fortune* (GH. *d*).—The Pagans, in general, held Fortune to be a goddefs, the ruler of all events, both good and bad. The Romans gave her feveral appellations, fuch as *Fortuna Libera, redux, publica, primigenia, equeſtris, parva, fors* or *fortis, virilis, feminea,* &c.[l]. but the two kinds of *Fortune,* which they chiefly diftinguifhed, were, the one *good* and the other *bad*; to the laft of which they probably addreffed themfelves in order to deprecate her ill-will.

Templum Fortunæ Primigeniæ, the temple of the *eldeſt,* or *firſt-born Fortune* (GH. *cd*). We find mention made [m] of a temple erected to this goddefs, by Servius Tullius, near the Capitol : but we cannot fay who erected this, which ftood between the *Viminal* and the *Efquiline* hills.

Templum Fortunæ Publicæ, the temple of *Public Fortune* (F. *cd*). This building ftood at the bottom of the Quirinal hill, near the way called *Viminalis* and *Nomentana*; but we know not by whom it was erected.

---

[l] For a more particular account of thefe feveral kinds of Fortune, worfhipped by the Romans, fee Rollin's Rom. Hift. Vol. I. p. 148 and 342. Vol. III. p. 294 Vol. IX. p. 259. and Crevier, Vol. I. p.106. Vol. VII. p. 244. and Vol. VIII. p. 143. [m] Rollin, Rom. Hift. Vol. I. p. 148.

Templum

Templum Fortunæ Virilis, the temple of *Virile*, or *Courageous Fortune* (AB. *e*) ; and another between CD. and *de*. fig. 240.—Ancus Martius, fourth king of the Romans, was the firſt man who built a temple at Rome, to this goddeſs ; with a deſign to intimate, ſay ſome writers, that courage is not leſs requiſite than good fortune, to obtain victories. If either of theſe buildings was that which *Ancus* built, we think it muſt have been the latter, upon the foundations of which now ſtands the Armenian church dedicated to *St. Mary of Egypt*.

Templum Herculis, the temple of *Hercules* (BC. *ef*); another, of the ſame (HI. *b*) ; and a third (C. *de*. 241), now a church dedicated to St. Stephen.

We alſo find an *Altar* dedicated to *Hercules*, by the name of *Ara maxima Herculis* (CD. *de*. 299), at the end of the Circus Maximus next the Tiber.

Templum & Ara Honoris, the temple and altar of *Honour* (H. *b*). This temple was built by an excellent architect called Mutius, by order of Marius, and might have been reckoned among the nobleſt buildings in ancient Rome, if the magnificence of the materials (which were only ſtone) had been anſwerable to the greatneſs of the deſign. It was particularly remarkable for this, that the entrance of it was dedicated to *Virtue*, and the reſt to *Honour* ; and that it had no *poſticum*, or back-door, as moſt other temples had ; thereby intimating, that we muſt not only paſs through virtue to attain to honour, but that honour is alſo obliged to repaſs through virtue ; that is, to perſevere therein, and acquire more of it.

Templum Jani, the temple of *Janus*, (CD. *d*. 259). The Romans, at different times, built three temples to *Janus*. In the firſt, erected by Romulus after he had made peace with the Sabines [a], ſtood a ſtatue of
Janus

[a] M. Rollin, Rom. Hiſt. Vol. I. p. 71. aſcribes the building of the firſt temple of *Janus*, to Numa, as an acknowledgment to the

D

Janus with two faces ; intimating, that the Romans and Sabines were united into one people, and that the two kings, Romulus and Tatius, made but one head to govern them. This temple was in the Roman *Forum* ; and Procopius fays, that in his time, the remains of it were ftill to be feen there, overagainft the Capitol, with a little niche of brafs, in which was a ftatue of *Janus*, of the fame metal, five feet high. Numa ordered that the gates of this temple, which were but two, fhould always be fhut in time of peace, and open in time of war ; ceremonies, which Virgil[o] has defcribed with a noble elegance : and accordingly when the conful, apointed to command the army, was ready to fet out, he went to this temple, attended by the fenate, the chief citizens, and his foldiers in their military dreffes, and opened it's gates. This ceremony was, indeed, very feldom performed ; the Romans being almoft continually engaged in wars. [p] The new confuls took poffeffion of their office in this temple ; whence they were faid to *open* the year.

The fecond temple of *Janus* was built by Cn. Duillius, in the *Forum Olitorum*, or herb-market, after the firft Carthaginian war ; and this, being fallen to decay, was rebuilt by the emperor Tiberius, according to Tacitus[q].

The third temple of *Janus*, here called *Templum Jani Augufti*, was fituated in the *Velabrum* (CD. *de.* 242), a little valley on one fide of the *Forum Boarium*, or ox-market, between the Capitol and mount Aventine. It was a fquare building, of the Ionic order, and entirely

---

the gods for the tranquility Rome enjoyed at his acceffion to the throne.

[o] Æn. 7. v. 607.

[p] For the times of opening and clofing this temple, fee Rollin's Rom. Hift. Vol. I. p.

71. IV. 168. XVI. 117. and Crevier's Rom. Emp. Vol. I. p. 56, 60, 209, 291. Vol. IV. p. 299. Vol. VI. p. 78, 340. and Vol. VIII. p. 417.

[q] Annal. l. 2.

of marble [y]. Marlianus [z], in whose time it still re-
mained almost entire, will not allow it to be so ancient as is pretended by some writers, who say, that
it was built by Numa, and repaired by Auguſtus.
This was the temple of *Janus Quadrifrons*, or *four-
faced Janus*; and owed it's origin, as well as name,
to the following accident, according to Servius. The
Romans, says he, after the taking of Faleria in Tuf-
cany, having met with a ſtatue of *Janus* that had
four faces, were deſirous to have ſuch a one at
Rome; and to honour him the more, they built him
a temple with four fronts, each having twelve
niches in it, with a great gate, which denoted the
four ſeaſons and the twelve months of the year.
Varro ſays there were alſo twelve altars in this temple
dedicated to *Janus*, each of which repreſented a month
of the year.

Templum Junonis, the temple of *Juno* (C. *de*), on
mount Aventine: and another of the ſame name on
the *Quirinal* hill (FG. *c*): but we know not by whom
either of theſe was erected.

Templum Junonis Monetæ, the temple of *Juno Mo-
neta* (CD. *de*. 255), ſo called *à monendo*, from her
having given ſalutary advice to the Romans [a] when
they were greatly diſtreſſed, either by the Gauls, or
by Pyrrhus; authors are not agreed which. It was
built in the year of Rome 410, M. Fabius Dorſo and
Servius Sulpicius Camerinus being conſuls [b], upon the
declivity of the Capitoline hill towards the Tiber.

Templum Junonis Soſpitæ, the temple of *Juno Soſ-
pita*; by which epithet is meant *the Giver or Preſerver of Health* [c]. This building ſtood on mount Palatine, not far from the Roman Forum (D. *de*).

[y] This ſeems to be the building of which we have a drawing
in the right hand corner of the
annexed plan.
[z] Topog. Rom. Antiq. l. 6.

c. 8.
[a] Cic. de Divin. l. 1. n. 101.
[b] Rollin. Rom. Hiſt. Vol.III.
p. 31.
[c] Cic. de Div. l. 1. n. 2.

Templum

Templum Junonis Reginæ, the temple of *Queen Juno*
(BC. *ef*) ; a fuperb ftructure, erected by the dictator
Camillus for a famous ftatue of this goddefs, which
he took in the city of Veii, and tranfported to
Rome [d].

Templum Jovis Cuftodis, the temple of *Jupiter the
Preferver* (CD. *de.* 265). This was one of the fixty
temples, that ftood upon the Capitoline hill. *Jupiter
Cuftos* was reprefented in it, holding his thunder with
one hand, and a dart with the other ; and the figure
of the emperor was either under his thunder, to fhew
that he was under *Jupiter's* protection ; or elfe en-
graved, laying upon a globe, and holding an image
of victory ; with the eagle at his feet, and thefe words,
Jovi Confervatori Auguftorum noftrorum. Very near
the fame place (at 262) is another temple dedicated to
Jupiter Cuftos and *Faith,* as we obferved before.

Templum Jovis Feretrii, the temple of *Jupiter Feretrius* (CD. *cd.* 261), built by Romulus upon the Capitoline hill, in order to depofit there the armour of
Acron, king of the Cæninenfes, whom he flew with
his own hand ; and to be a repofitory for any future
fpoils of the fame kind, which were called *opima fpolia.*
The epithet *Feretrius* was derived from the Latin
word *Feretrum,* which we find ufed by Livy, to fig-
nify the trophy carried by Romulus on this occafion [e].

Templum Jovis Optimi Maximi, likewife called the
temple of *Jupiter Capitolinus,* and, moft commonly,
the *Capitol* (CD. *de.* 236). This building was the
effect of a vow made by the elder Tarquin in the Sabine war [f]: but he had fcarce laid the foundation of it
before his death. His nephew, Tarquin the Proud,
finifhed it with the fpoils taken from the neighbouring

[d] We have a full and curious
account of this tranfaction in M.
Rollin's Rom. Hift. Vol. II.
p. 271—276.

[e] See Rollin's Rom. Hift.
Vol. I. p. 44.

[f] Livy, l. 1. See alfo Rollin's Rom. Hift. Vol. I. p. 138.

nations,

·nations[s]. But upon the expulfion of the kiñgs, the .confecration of the building was performed by the conful *Horatius*[b]. This ftructure ftood upon a high hill, called *Mons Capitolinus*, and took in four acres of ground. The front was adorned with three rows of pillars: the other fides with two[i]. There were three chapels in it: that of Jupiter in the middle; that of Minerva on the right hand, near the place where the nail was driven in annually, to reckon the number of years; and that of Juno on the left. The afcent to it was by an hundred fteps[k]. The prodigious gifts and ornaments, with which it was endowed at different times, almoft exceed belief. Suetonius[l] tells us, that Auguftus gave to it at once two thoufand pounds weight of gold: and in jewels and precious ftones, to the value of five hundred *feftertia*. Livy and Pliny[m] furprife us with accounts of the brazen threfholds; the noble pillars that *Sylla* removed thither from the temple of *Jupiter Olympius* at Athens; the gilded roof; the gilded fhields, and thofe of folid filver; the huge veffels of filver; the golden chariot; and many other valuable things with which this temple was enriched. It was firft confumed by fire in the Marian war, and then rebuilt by Sylla, who, dying before the dedication, left that honour to Quintus Catulus[n]. This too was demolifhed in the *Vitellian* fedition[o]. Vefpafian built it anew a third time, and confecrated it with great ceremony[p]: but this alfo was burnt about the time of his death. Domitian raifed the laft, and moft magnificent of all, in which

[s] Liv. ibid. and Rollin, Vol.I. p. 177.
[b] Plut. in Poplicol.
[i] Dionyf. Halicarnaf.
[k] Tacit.
[l] In Auguft. c. 30.
[m] Liv. l. 35, 38. Plin. l. 33, &c.

[n] See Rollin, Vol. X. p. 106 and 139.
[o] See Crevier's Rom. Emp. Vol. V. p. 312.
[p] Of which we have a particular account in Crevier's Rom. Emp. Vol. VI. p. 32.

the

the gilding alone coft twelve thoufand talents [p] : on which account Plutarch [q] has obferved of that emperor, that he was, like Midas, defirous of turning every thing into gold. In this temple vows were made, and folemn oaths; here the citizens ratified the acts of the emperors, and fwore fealty to them, and hither the magiftrates, and the generals that triumphed, came to give thanks to the gods for the victories they had obtained, and to pray for the profperity of the empire. The now very fmall remains of this building are converted into a Chriftian church, dedicated to the virgin Mary, under the appellation of *Sancta Maria in Ara Cæli* [r].

Templum Jovis Statoris, the temple of *Jupiter Stator* (D. *de.* 267). Romulus, feeing his men give way in a battle againft the Sabines commanded by their king Tatius, and already in poffeffion of the Capitol, prayed to Jupiter to ftop them, and vowed, if his requeft was granted, to build a temple to him in that very place, as a monument that Rome was faved by his protection. The Romans rallied and defeated their enemies; and Romulus acquitted himfelf of his engagement, by erecting, at the foot of the Capitoline hill, this temple, which he dedicated to his god under the name of *Stator*; an epithet derived from the Latin word *fiftere, to ftop* [s]. Piranefi has given a drawing of fome of the pillars of this temple, which ftill remain.

Templum Jovis Tonantis, the temple of *Jupiter the Thunderer* (CD. *d.* 250). As Auguftus was marching againft the Cantabrians, the thunder fell near his litter in the night, and killed one of his fervants, who carried a torch : whereupon that emperor vowed a temple to *Jupiter Tonans,* for having preferved him

[p] Plut. in Poplicol. See alfo nat. Nardini, & alii.
Crevier, Vol. VI. p. 317.   [s] See alfo Rollin's Rom. Hift.
[q] Ibid.   Vol. I. p. 47, & feq.
[r] Fabricii Roma, c. 9. Do-

in

in fo great a danger ʹ. He accordingly built this, at the foot of the Capitoline hill, with fuch magnificence of ftructure and elegance of tafte, as, if we may judge from it's few remaining pillars of Oriental marble, now greatly funk into the ground, fhew the vaft perfection to which the polite arts were carried in the Auguftan age ᵘ. *Fortune* is here added to the appellation of this temple.

Templum Jovis Victoris, the temple of *Jupiter the Conqueror* (CD. *de.* 273); erected by the conful L. Papyrius Curfor, for his victory over the Gauls and Samnites ᵂ, in the year of Rome 459.

Befides thefe temples erected to Jupiter, under various appellations, we have, in this plan, a chapel dedicated to him and Minerva, *Sacellum Jovis & Minervæ*, between the letters F and G, and over againft *c*.

Templum Liberi (CD. *ef*), and, near the fame fpot, *Templum Liberæ* ; both almoft adjoining to the *Circus Maximus.—Liber* was one of the epithets given to Bacchus ; either becaufe he procured the Bœotians their liberty ; or becaufe he is the god of wine, and drinking gives a temporary eafe to difturbed minds. We find on the confular medals of the family of Caffia, reprefentations of *Liber* and *Libera*, as they are called in ancient infcriptions ; that is, of male and female *Bacchus :* and Tacitus inform us ˣ, that Tiberius repaired and dedicated anew, the temples of *Liber* and *Libera*, which time and other accidents had greatly damaged.

" As for the myfteries of *Liber*, fays St. Auguftine ʸ,
" whom they (the heathens) have made to prefide
" over the feminal powers of liquids, I mean, not
" only over the juices of fruits, among which wine
" has the pre-eminence, but alfo over the feed of ani-

ᵗ Sueton. in Auguft. and Crevier, Vol. I. p. 369.

ᵘ Piranefi has given a noble drawing of the remains of this temple in his Views of Rome.

ᵂ See Rollin's Rom. Hift. Vol. III. p. 283—293.

ˣ Annal. l. 2.

ʸ De Civitat. Dei, l. 7. c. 21.

" mals ;

" mals ; I am loth to take notice of the excefs of in-
" famy they arrived to therein ; but yet I muft fay
" (in order to confound the arrogant ftupidity of our
" adverfaries), though I am obliged to omit many
" other things upon this occafion, becaufe they are too
" tedious ; that, according to the teftimony of Varro,
" the feafts of *Liber* were celebrated with fo much
" licentioufnefs in fome places in Italy, that, in ho-
" nour of him, they gave adoration to the privy
" parts of man, and that not in fecret to cover their
" fhame, but publickly to make wickednefs appear
" triumphant : for they placed him after an honour-
" able manner in a chariot, which was brought into
" the city after they had firft drawn it through the
" fields. But at Lavinium they fpent a whole month
" in celebrating the feafts of *Liber* only, during which
" time, there all imaginable impurity of fpeech was
" encouraged, until the faid chariot had traverfed the
" market-place, and was brought whither the peo-
" ple defigned to depofit what they carried : after
" which, the moft virtuous ladies in the city muft go
" and crown this infamous thing, before the multi-
" tude. In this manner it was that they made the
" god *Liber* favourable to feeds, and expelled charms
" and witchcraft out of the earth."

Templum Libertatis, the temple of *Liberty* (C. *e*) ;
built, according to Dion Caffius[g], upon mount
Aventine, on the very fpot where Cicero's houfe once
ftood, enriched with feveral brafs pillars, and numbers of fine ftatues.

Templum Martis, the temple of *Mars* (D. *de*. 167),
on the declivity of the Capitoline hill ; built by Auguftus to the god *Mars*, with the addition of the
epithet of *Ultor, the Avenger*[h], in confequence of a
vow made by him in the Philippic war, and of

[g] Lib. 43.
[h] See Crevier's Rom. Emp. Vol. I. p. 96.

the fuppofed affiftance of this deity in helping him to revenge the death of Julius Cæfar. The eagles, and other military enfigns of the Romans, were kept in this temple, which was of a round form ; as was alfo, by order of the fenate, the chariot in which Cæfar had triumphed [i]. We have another of the fame fhape, and dedicated to the fame god, juft without the walls of Rome, near the Latine gate ; under the letter E, and betwen g and b.

Templum Matris Deorum, the temple of *the Mother of the Gods* (D. *de*). The Romans had no knowledge of this deity, which we find called by the various names of *Cybele, Ops, Rhea, Idæ Mater*, &c. till the year of Rome 547, in the confulfhip of P. Cornelius Scipio, afterwards furnamed *Africanus*, and P. Licinius Craffus, when a fhower of large hail, miftaken for ftones, fell, and greatly alarmed the people during the fecond Punic war. They had recourfe to the books of the Sibyls ; which telling them, that in order to drive their enemies out of Italy, they muft bring the mother of the gods from Peffinuntum to Rome, they difpatched ambaffadors to Attalus king of Phrygia, and he delivered to them the goddefs, who was reprefented by a thick, fhapelefs, rough ftone. M. Valerius, one of the deputies, being arrived at Teracina with this ftone, fent notice of it to the fenate, telling them, that it was neceffary to depute, together with a number of ladies, the beft man in the city, to receive her. The confcript fathers pitched upon P. Cornelius Scipio Nafica, who, with the Roman ladies, went to receive her at Oftia, and brought her to Rome, where they placed her in the temple of Victory, upon mount Palatine. The cenfors, M. Livius and Claudius, built a temple for her the next year, and M. Junius Brutus dedicated it thirteen years after [k].

[i] Dio, l. 50.
[k] See Rollin's Rom. Hift. Vol. VI. p. 181—184, for a particular, and very fenfible account of this tranfaction.

Templum

Templum Mercurii, the temple of *Mercury* (CD. *ef*), near the Circus Maximus. . We cannot say by whom this temple was built. The Greeks and Romans sacrificed a calf to this deity ; and made him oblations of milk and honey, as to the god of sweet eloquence. Callistratus and Homer say, it was a custom to present him neat's-tongues, by throwing them into the fire, and sprinkling them with wine, because he was the god of speech, of which the tongue is the organ. The Germans, according to Tacitus, worshipped him as the sovereign of the gods, and offered him human sacrifices. The Greeks erected statues to him, which they placed before their houses, and the Romans set up others of the same kind in their cross-ways and high-roads. These statues, called *Hermæ*, had neither arms nor legs, and were a quite shapeless lump of matter, excepting that they had a head.

Templum Minervæ, the temple of *Minerva* (DE. *ef*), near the Circus Maximus ; and another (D. *gh*), just without the walls of Rome, upon the borders of mount Aventine, probably that which Ovid speaks of[k], as a most magnificent structure.

Templum Deæ Neniæ, the temple of the goddess *Nenia* (HI. *c*), who presided over the dirges or mournful tunes sung at the burying of the dead[m]. This temple stood just without the gate *Nomentana*, now *St. Agnes :* and a little farther was a grove, in which it was customary to sacrifice a red-haired dog (whence the name *Catularia*) and a sheep, towards the beginning of April ; the former to the Dog-star,

---

[k] Fast. l. 6.

[l] *Nenia* is derived from a Hebrew word, which signifies *lamentation* or *complaint*. Those elegant pieces, the lamentations of Jeremy upon the destruction of the Jewish mo-

narchy and the city of Jerusalem, and David's mourning for the death of Saul and Jonathan, were, properly, *Neniæ*. The *Neniæ* for the dead began immediately after the party expired.

that

that it might not parch the corn upon the ground; and the latter to *Mildew* [m] (*Rubigo*) that it might not blight it.

Templum Opis & Saturni, the temple of *Ops* and *Saturn* (CD. *de*, 257), two of the firſt gods of the Latines. The Romans gave the name of *Ops* to the earth. This temple ſtood upon the Capitoline hill, near thoſe of Jupiter *Cuſtos*, and Jupiter *Stator*.

Templum Pacis, the temple of *Peace* (DE. *de*), begun by the emperor Claudius, and finiſhed by Veſpaſian, who not only embelliſhed it with paintings and ſtatues of the greateſt maſters, but likewiſe depoſited in this building all the ſpoils and riches taken by his ſon Titus in the temple of Jeruſalem [n]. It was burnt in the reign of Commodus [o]. Piraneſi has given us an elegant drawing of the ruins that now remain of this once magnificent temple.

The *Pantheon* (CD. *c*. 90), built by M. Agrippa, ſon-in-law of Auguſtus [p], and dedicated by him to *Jupiter the Avenger*, acording to Pliny's account ; and to *Mars*, *Venus*, and *Julius Cæſar*, according to Dion Caſſius [q]: but the moſt probable opinion is, that it was dedicated to *all the Gods*, as it's very name (*quaſi τῶν πάντων Θεῶν*) implies. This ſtruct̆ure, according to Fabricius [r], is an hundred and forty feet high, and about as much in breadth. The roof is curiouſly vaulted, void ſpaces being left here and there for greater ſtrength. The rafters, forty feet long, were plated with braſs. There are no windows in the whole edifice : but a very ſufficient light is let in through a round hole in the top of the roof. The walls of the Pantheon are eighteen feet thick [s] and either of ſolid marble, or incruſted on the in-

[m] Ovid, Faſt. 4.
[n] See Crevier, Vol. VI. p. 81 and 97.
[o] Id. Vol. VII. p. 400.
[p] See Crevier, Vol. I. p. 54
and 55.
[q] Lib. 1. c. 2.
[r] Roma, c. 9.
[s] Nodor, Relation de la Cour de Rome, p. 460.

ſide :

fide [t]: the outfide of the front was formerly covered
with plates of brafs gilt, and the top with plates of
filver; in lieu of which there now is lead [u]. The
gates were of brafs, of extraordinary fize and work-
manfhip [w].

This temple, which was damaged by a great fire
in the reign of Titus [x], and afterwards repaired and
beautified by Adrian [y] and Severus [z], is ftill ftanding,
with little alteration, except the lofs of it's old ornaments, and that inftead of afcending to it by
twelve fteps, as formerly, the fame number is now
defcended at it's entrance. Pope Boniface the Fourth,
who begged this building of the emperor Phocas,
changed it's ancient name, by dedicating it to *the
virgin Mary and all the faints* [a]. It is now generally
called *Santa Maria della Rotonda* [b]: the epithet *rotonda* being taken from it's circular from. We have a
view of this edifice in the left hand corner of the
annexed plan.

Templum Penatum, the temple of the *Houfhold Gods*
(DE. *ef*); near the Circus Maximus. The *Dii Penates* were worfhipped by the ancients in their houfes,
and looked upon as the fouls, or *Genii* of deceafed
perfons belonging to the particular families. Thefe
gods were honoured within doors, by burning, in the
nature of firft fruits, part of each thing that was
ferved to the table; or by publickly facrificing a fow
to them, as to thofe who prefided over the ftreets and
high-ways. There were alfo the public *Penates* of the
city and empire, which Æneas brought from Troy,
and which Varro believed to have been carried thither
from Samothrace. The temple here mentioned was
that of thefe public *Penates*. A light was continually
burnt before the *Penates*, to whom libations and in-

[t] Marlian. l. 6. c. 6.   [z] Id. Vol. VIII. p. 134.
[u] Id. & Fabric. c. 9.   [a] See the Hift. of the Popes,
[w] Marlian. l. 6. c. 6.   publifhed by J. Mills, Vol. I.
[x] See Crevier, Vol. V. p. 295. p. 396.
[y] Id. Vol. VII. p. 154.   [b] Id. & Fabric. c. 9.

cenfe

cenfe were offered upon almoft all occafions. Lucan obferves, that, in time of peace, the Romans ufed to hang up their arms in the place appertaining to their houfhold gods, as intrufting them to their keeping; and that it was efteemed an abominable facrilege to commit murder in the prefence of *Vefta*, that is, in the entry, and before the perpetual fire of the houfhold gods.

Templum Quietis, the temple of *Reft* (F. *ef*): by whom built, or what were the rites peculiar to this temple, we know not.

Templum Quirini, the temple of *Quirinus* (FG. *c.* 294), upon the *Quirinal* hill; and again (GH. *b*) without the walls, between the gates *Pinciana* and *Salaria*. *Quirinus* was a furname of Romulus, who was fo called from *Quiris*, a fort of javelin which the Sabines ufed, according to Feftus; or from the Sabines themfelves, who were called *Cures*; or from the god Mars, who was called *Quiris*, and from whom Romulus was faid to be defcended. The former of thefe temples was decreed by the fenate immediately after the death of Romulus[c]; and the latter was confecrated by the dictator L. Papirius Curfor, in the year of Rome 459[d].

Templum Romuli & Remi, the temple of *Romulus* and *Remus* (C. *de*) upon mount Aventine. We cannot fay when, or by whom, this edifice was built.

Templum Saturni, the temple of *Saturn*, of which we find three in this plan, *viz.* (D. *de.* 168),—(CD. *de*, 237), — and (CD. *de.* 238). The firft temple of Saturn was erected by Tatius king of the Sabines, after the peace concluded between him and Romulus: the fecond was confecrated by Tullus Hoftilius, after he had triumphed three times over the Sabines, and twice over the Albans; at which time he likewife inftituted the *Saturnalia*: and the third was dedi-

[c] Rollin, Rom. Hift. Vol. I.   [d] Id. Vol. III. p. 293. p. 61.

cated

cated by the confuls A. Sempronius Atratinus, and
M. Minutius.   One of thefe temples, but we cannot
fay precifely which, was the place where the public
money, and the records and regifters of the ftate
were kept ; and alfo the place where foreign ambaffadors were firft received by the public treafurers, who
fet down their names in the regifters of the treafury,
and defrayed their expences.   There too the names
of all the citizens were inrolled ; and flaves, who had
obtained their freedom, went thither, and hung up
their chains.

Templum Serapis, the temple of *Serapis* (CD. *ef*),
and (GH. *c*), an Egyptian deity, the worfhip of
which is faid to have been introduced at Rome
by Adrian, after his return from Alexandria.
Serapis is thought to be the fame with the
fun.

Templum Solis Aureliani, Aurelian's temple of the
Sun (DE. *cd*), upon the *Quirinal* hill.   The Phœni-
cians called the fun *Elagabal,* from whence came the
name of *Heliogabalus,* given to the emperor *Antoninus,*
who was prieft of that planet, to which he erected a
temple on mount *Palatine,* and would have removed
thither not only all the facrifices of the Romans, but
alfo thofe of the Jews[*].

Templum Solis & Lunæ, the temple of the *Sun* and
Moon (DE. *de*. 287) ; fuppofed, by fome, to have
been alfo called *Ifis & Serapis* We have an accurate
drawing of the fmall remains of this temple, in Piranefi's *Views of Rome.*

Templum Dei Sylvani, the temple of the god *Sylvanus* (EF. *c*), who, fay the poets, prefided over
forefts and land-marks.   Some call him the fon of
Faunus ; but Plutarch, in his Parallels, will have
him to have been begotten inceftuoufly by Valerius,
on his daughter Valeria.   Feneftella fays, that *Pan,*

[*] See the life of Heliogabalus, in Crevier, Vol.VIII. p. 228,
& feq.

Faunus,

Faunus, and *Sylvanus,* were the fame deity. The *Luperci* were their priefts, and their feafts the *Lupercalia.*

Templum Telluris, the temple of the *Earth* (GH. *ef*), which the Romans worfhipped both as a god and a goddefs, by the names of *Tellus* and *Tellumo.* *Tellus* was the female, and fuppofed to receive and nourifh the feeds which came from the male *Tellumo.*

Templum Veneris, the temple of *Venus* (CD. *ef*), near the Circus Maximus; fuppofed, by fome, to have been erected by Auguftus to *Venus Genetrix,* or *Venus the Mother*[f].

Templum Veneris & Cupidinis, the temple of *Venus and Cupid* (GH. *fg*), in the angle within the walls of Rome, near the gate *Nævia.*

Templum Veneris Erycinæ, the temple of *Venus Erycina* (HI. *ab*), near the *Via Salaria,* without the walls of Rome.

Templum Veneris Erycinæ & Mentis, the temple of *Venus Erycina and the Mind* (CD. *d.* 253), upon the Capitoline hill, and near the *Via Capitolina;* but by whom built, or on what occafion, is more than we can fay.

Simulacrum Veneris Verticordiæ (H. *ab*). In the year of Rome 627, the fenate, afflicted at the great depravity of the Romans, confulted the books of the Sibyls, for a remedy; and, in confequence of the anfwer they were fuppofed to give, refolved that a temple fhould be erected to *Venus,* under the new furname of *Verticordia,* which implied, that fhe was invoked to *turn the heart.* It was alfo added, that a ftatue of *Venus* fhould be placed and dedicated in this temple, by the moft virtuous woman in Rome: a fingular regulation, in a matter not a little delicate. In confequence of this, the ladies themfelves nominated an hundred from amongft them; and out of

[f] See Rollin's Rom. Hift. Vol. XIV. p. 197.

E   this

this hundred, ten were chosen by lot, who unani-
mously singled out Sulpicia, the daughter of Sulpicius Paterculus, and wife of Q. Fulvius Flaccus [g].
This is very like the chusing of Scipio Nasica, as
the worthiest and most upright man among the Romans, to fetch the mother of the gods from Pessi-
nuntum in Phrygia, as we have already mentioned.

Templum Vertumni, the temple of *Vertumnus* (CD. de.
271), near the *Forum Boarium*, or Ox-market. *Vertumnus* was the god of gardens, and also an emblem of the
year. He was worshipped under a thousand various
forms: for which reason Horace says, *Vertumnis
natus iniquis*, as if there were as many different
Vertumni, as there were different forms by which
this deity was represented. The Greeks called him
Proteus.

Templum Vestæ, T. Dei Panis, & T. Eliogabali ;
the temple of *Vesta, Pan*, and *Heliogabalus* (DE. e.
279). How these three came to be joined here, we
know not. *Vesta*, according to Ennius, or Entæme-
rus, quoted by Lactantius, was the wife of Uranus,
the father of Saturn, the first that reigned in the
world. This genealogy is like that of Sanchoniatho,
excepting that he calls the earth the wife of Uranus,
which we know has been confounded with *Vesta*.
Vesta passed from Phœnicia into Greece, where, Dio-
dorus Siculus says, she was looked upon as the
daughter of Saturn and Rhea, and the first inven-
tress of architecture. However, it is not to be
doubted, but that *Vesta* was every where also taken
for a goddess of nature, under whose name the
earth and fire were worshipped, rather than for an
historical goddess. Ovid says, that *Vesta* was the
daughter of Saturn and Rhea, as well as Juno and
Ceres: that these two last married, but that *Vesta*
continued a virgin, and barren, as fire is pure and

[g] See Rollin's Rom. Hist. Vol. IX. p. 106.

barren.

barren. The same poet adds, that the perpetual fire was the only representation they had of *Vesta*; the true image of fire being not to be given; and that it was the custom of the ancients to keep fire at the entrance of their houses, which from thence retained the name of *Vestibulum*, or *Vestibule*. The *Vestal* virgins were the priestesses of this goddess.

THEATRES and AMPHITHEATRES.

The *Theatres* of the Romans, borrowed from those of the Greeks, were semi-circular, and designed for dramatic entertainments. Their *Amphitheatres*, intended for the greater shews of gladiators, wild beasts, &c. were round, or, more generally, oval, like two *Theatres* joined together [a]. The principal divisions of these buildings were the *Scena*, *Proscenium*, and *Area*, of which the classic authors make frequent mention.

The *Scena* was a partition reaching quite cross the theatre, being either *versatilis* or *ductilis*, to turn round, or draw up, in order to present a new prospect to the spectators [b].

The *Proscenium* was the space just before the scene, where the actors performed [c].

The middle part, or *Area* of the *Amphitheatre*, was called *Cavea*, because it was considerably lower than the rest (whence perhaps the name of *Pit* in our playhouses;) and *Area*, because it used to be strown with sand, to hinder the combatants from slipping.

The seats were distinguished according to the ordinary division of the people into senators, knights, and commons. The first range was called *Orchestra* [d]; the second *Equestria*; the third *Popularia* [e].

[a] Polydor. Virg. de Rer. invent. l. 3. c. 13.
[b] Serv. in Georg. 3.
[c] Rosin. lib 5. c. 4.
[d] From ὀρχεῖσθαι; because the dances were performed in that part of the Grecian theatres.
[e] Casalius de Urb. Rom. & Imp. Splend. lib. 2. c. 5.

☞ In the firſt ages of the commonwealth, the theatres of the Romans were only temporary, and built of wood, ſo ſlightly, that they ſometimes fell down with great deſtruction ; of which we have a remarkable inſtance in that of *Fidenæ*, which maimed, or cruſhed to death, fifty thouſand ſpectators [f].

The moſt magnificent of theſe moveable, or temporary, theatres, was that of *M. Scaurus*, mentioned by Pliny [g], and deſcribed at large by M. Rollin [h]. Pompey the Great was the firſt that raiſed a fixed theatre at Rome, which he built very nobly with hewn ſtone, and for which he was ſeverely cenſured, as introducing a new cuſtom [i].

The remains of this theatre of Pompey are ſtill to be ſeen at Rome, as are alſo thoſe of ſome others: but we ſhall confine ourſelves here to the three following, noticed in this plan : *viz.*

The *Coliſeum* (DE. *e*), called alſo, by corruption, *Coloſſeum, quaſi à Coloſſo*, ſays Philander, from a coloſſal ſtatue of Nero, which ſtood near it. This *Amphitheatre*, of which there ſtill are moſt ſtately remains (finely drawn by Piraneſi), was built by Veſpaſian, and dedicated by his ſon Titus ; whence it is alſo called ſometimes the *Flavian*, and ſometimes *Titus's* amphitheatre: It's ſituation, as Suetonius obſerves [k], and as we ſee by this plan, was nearly in the middle of the city. M. Crevier deſcribes it in the ſixth volume of his hiſtory of the Roman Emperors [l].

The amphitheatre of *Statilius Taurus* (GH. *fg*), built, in the reign of Auguſtus, by *Statilius Taurus*, prefect of Rome [m].

---

[f] See Crevier, Vol. II. p. 291.

[g] Lib. 36. c. 15.

[h] Rom. Hiſt. Vol. III. p. 16. and Vol. XII. p. 156.

[i] Tacit. Ann. 14. and Rollin, Rom. Hiſt. Vol. III. p. 20, 22. and Vol. XII. p. 325.

[k] In Tito, c. 7.

[l] Page 296.

[m] See Crevier's Rom. Emp. Vol. I. p. 33.

Marcellus's

Marcellus's Theatre (C. *d.* 228), built by Auguſtus in honour of his nephew *Marcellus*[n].   The remains of this *Theatre*, finely repreſented by Piraneſi, are, as Fabricius obſerves [o], by far the moſt perfeᴄt of any of the ancient Roman buildings.

The Romans had alſo another kind of public edifice, called *Odeum* [p], much after the manner of a *Theatre*, where the muſicians and aᴄtors rehearſed their parts before their appearance on the ſtage [q].   Plutarch [r] gives the following deſcription of one of their *Odea* at Athens, from whence the Romans undoubtedly took the hint of theirs.   " In the inſide, ſays he, " it was full of ſeats and ranges of pillars; and on " the outſide, the roof, or covering, was made from " a point at top, with a great many bendings, all " ſhelving downward, in imitation of a Perſian pa- " vilion."

T O M B S.

The tombs mentioned in this plan, are,

Adrian's Tomb, now the caſtle of *St. Angelo* (C. *b*).

Auguſtus's Tomb or *Mauſoleum* (DE.*b.* 48.)

That of *C. Ceſtius*, in the form of a pyramid, much noticed by antiquarians, near the gate *Trigemina* [s] (BC. *fg*).

The ſepulchre of the *Domitian* family (EF. *bc*).

That of *Nero* (DE. *ab*) ; and that of

Scipio Africanus (BC. *ab.* 15).

Under this head we may alſo, not improperly, notice,

[n] Crevier, Vol. I. p. 226.

[o] Rom. c. 12.

[p] Fabric. Rom. c. 12.

[q] Roſin. l. 5. c. 4.

[r] In Pericle.

[s] See Donatus and Nardini, and Crevier, Vol. VII. p. 156. Nardini has given correᴄt drawings of this tomb, in his *Roma Antica*; and Piraneſi has given an elegant one, in his Views of Rome.

The

The place where the dead bodies of the Roman citizens were burnt, *L. Uſt. Civium* (HI. *d*), and the trench in which their bones were afterwards buried, *Foſſa in quam projiciebant oſſa cadaverum uſtorum* (HI. *de*): though we are apt to think that the former of theſe is marked ſomewhat wrong in this plan [u]; a law of the Romans expreſsly forbidding any dead body to be burnt, or buried, within the walls of the city.

TROPHIES.

The deſign of trophies needs no explication : nor can the ſhape of them be better deſcribed than it is in Virgil's ſecond Æneid.

Of thoſe which Marius raiſed after the *Cimbric* war, ſtill remaining at Rome, we have this account in Fabricius [w] : " They are two trunks of marble " hung round with ſpoils. One of them is covered " with a ſcaly corſlet, with ſhields and other military " ornaments. Juſt before it is ſet a young man in " the poſture of a captive, with his hands tied be- " hind him ; and all round were winged images of " victory. The other is ſet out with the common " military garb ; having a ſhield of an unequal " round, and two helmets, one open and adorned " with creſts, the other cloſe without creſts. On " the ſame trophy is the ſhape of a ſoldier's coat, " with ſeveral other deſigns, which, by reaſon of " the decay of the marble, are very difficult to be " diſcovered."

Theſe two trophies now adorn the front of the preſent Capitol.

[u] Unleſs the walls of the city are extended here beyond what they were in the time of ancient Rome ; which is the opinion of

J. B. Donius, in his ingenious Treatiſe *De reſtituenda Salubritate Agri Romani.*
[w] Cap. 14.

www.ingramcontent.com/pod-product-compliance
Lightning Source LLC
Chambersburg PA
CBHW030022030726
47499CB00008B/3085